I0664756

The Man That Got Away

an illustrated confession

Jameson Currier

Chelsea Station

Editions

Chelsea Station Editions

New York

The Man That Got Away
story and art by Jameson Currier

Copyright © 2024 by Jameson Currier.

All rights reserved.

No part of this book may be reproduced in any form without written permission from the publisher, except by a reviewer, who may quote brief passages in a review where appropriate credit is given; nor may any part of this book be reproduced, stored in a retrieval system, or transmitted in any form or by any means—electronic, photocopying, recording, or other—without specific written permission from the publisher.

The Man That Got Away by Jameson Currier is entirely a work of fiction. Any references to historical events, real people, or real places are used fictitiously. Other names, characters, places, and events are product of the author's imagination, and any resemblance to actual events, places or persons, living or dead, is entirely coincidental.

Cover and book design by Peachboy Distillery & Designs

Published by Chelsea Station Editions
www.chelseastationeditions.com
New York, NY

Print ISBN: 978-0-9844707-6-1
Ebook ISBN: 978-1-937627-37-9
Library of Congress Control Number: 2024908926

First Edition

The Man That Got Away
an illustrated confession by
Jameson Currier

A mesmerizing tale of a young man's education by drag queens, a fatal accident and its cover-up, and the resulting aftermath on lives and friendships, as told through archived documents.

Praise for the writings of Jameson Currier

"A writer who consistently surprises and delights, Currier's dynamism will surely carry his literary career to higher heights."
—*Bay Area Reporter*

"The breadth of Currier's personal experience is evident in his writing, which is moving without resorting to melodrama, familiar without feeling clichéd."
—*Windy City Times*

"As a writer, Currier should be lauded for his creative decision to avoid the all-too-common formulaic trappings of most current novels written for and about gay men."
—*Lambda Literary*

"Currier has an incredible knack for portraying gay men as complex and flawed yet like-minded, mostly likable and relatable individuals."
—*Edge*

Also by Jameson Currier

The Man That Got Away

To all the queens and divas,
past, present, and forever

I first heard a part of this story one night in 1980 when I met Billy Goodman at the opening night party of an off-Broadway show I was working on. At the time, I was apprenticing as a theatrical publicist and Billy was writing scenes for a daily soap opera that was filming in New York City, and Billy thought his anecdotes about his drag queen friends in Atlanta might be the spark of a stage musical or a screenplay, but he expressed a hesitancy of tackling the idea. Our tête-à-tête over the next few weeks revealed a lot of similarities between us—we were both from Georgia; we had both fled overbearing, religious families; and we both had an obsessive love of the theater. I regretted that we let things slip between us in the way that things do in Manhattan circles—other commitments, other invitations, and an interest in other men. I always thought there was something right about us together and that if we had tried, really tried, we might have made a perfect couple. But we were both young—still in our twenties—and had many more adventures ahead of us.

A year later Billy's play, *The Augmented Third*, was presented off-Broadway, and Billy convinced his producers to take a chance on hiring a young publicist to flog his words and ideas to an unsuspecting public. I was grateful for the work and promised Billy that one day he would not be sorry for it. Our friendship continued long after the run of that play and I often asked him if he was at work on something about his "drag queens back home," though he usually answered that he was swamped by another project.

But Billy was at work on a tale about his drag friends in Atlanta, a nonfiction account, though it would not see publication until after his death in 1998, after a long battle with AIDS. When I finally read the draft of this story, I understood Billy's hesitation to talk with me in detail about this moment in his life. When his account was published, the publisher of the magazine categorized it as fiction since many facts could not confirmed and to avoid further investigation into the crime it detailed.

I am indebted to Billy's longtime partner, Sean Burke, for sorting through Billy's boxes of correspondence and reams of keepsakes to find all of the elements to include with Billy's confession of the cover-up of a crime.

This edition went through many drafts and there were many conversations over the documents that are included in this book. Publication was delayed due to legal review, but the lapse of time allowed new information to be discovered. In 2014, after visiting Billy's sister in Georgia because the family home was being sold, Sean arrived to his own conclusions about the truth of Billy's tale of a cover-up in the deep South. I am indebted and honored to be able to include his theory in the Afterword to this edition, along with the remarkable portraits Sean created to illustrate Billy's tale. Sean's continued pursuit to know the truth about his partner and maintain the memory of Billy's work is the beating heart behind this story.

Jameson Currier
June 2024

The following is a reproduction of an original document archived in the William B. Goodman Papers, Special Collections, Hayes Research Center, New York Public Library. Opinions expressed are those of the author of the letter. Copyright held by The Cheshire Bridge Legacy Project, Inc., as beneficiary of the Estate of David W. Duffy, and reprinted by permission.

THE PEACHTREE ARMS APARTMENTS
WEST PEACHTREE STREET
ATLANTA, GA 30303

April 16, 1990

My dearest Billy,

I have tried several times reaching you at your Manhattan boudoir and all I seem to get is that infernal answering machine, except for last week when I shared a brief (but still lovely) conversation with your Significant Other. Mary, does that Big Fella do testosterone injections? His voice is so low and grumbly that I wished Mr. Bell had invented a way to tele-transport me right over to him so I could check out his assets. I'm certain he is a handful — he certainly sounded like he is a mouthful, and from that I must deduce he might be one of the legitimate reasons why you don't return my call with the haste it deserves—he must keep you awfully busy (or at least on your knees most of the time). But, Darling Dearest, he didn't seem to know who I am, or who I am to you, and herein lies my reason to write you: to remind you of all the things that were lovely and special during your youthful

Is Billy there? ♡

He's tied up right now!

Atlanta adventures, which you shouldn't forget about. Are you ashamed of your ancient Southern history and all your beautiful and lovely sisters from Lady Belle's with whom you were so well acquainted in your Auntie Bella homeland? Is that the reason why I did not see your lovely smile and sorry ass in Hot Lanta for Miss Sincerely Peaches' Celebration of Life?

Yes, dearest, Peaches has now gone on to that fully-stocked, custom-designed gilded dressing room on Cloud Number Nine. Peaches was valiant and strong and courageous and brave, and yes, even beautiful, right up to the end, I can assure you of that, since I was there to witness all the proud and, yes, painful details firsthand. She was down to skin and bones and less than 120 pounds; her skin was so pale her veins looked like rivers of pearls. She carried her vanity right to the end, I want you to know. She was never a stubbly mess like some of the others I have been there to assist at the final moments. (Peaches had an electric razor at her bedside that she could manipulate even when she could not punch the buttons on the tiny remote control of her deluxe widescreen color TV.) Even at the final end she was a vision of beauty. I was there, Sweetie, with a water glass and tissues in hand — keeping that fruity Eva Gabor wig on straight when she stretched her hands up to receive Our Great Lady in the Sky. Only the night before had we refreshed her nails — stripped off her signature Peach Blossom Pink and painted them with a clear varnish, so that when Her Divine Holiness came to take her away from us, she would be as pure and virginal as a sister with her sordid background could hope to be.

So, of course, Peaches' Celebration of a Life Lived with Ultra-Glamour was a great and grand affair, a truly historical moment — all the Spectacular Sisters from the heydays of the Legacy were reunited for one great big bitchfest. (Even Lady Belle herself showed up with her flaming bloodshot eyes and retro movie-star attire.) Peaches had been planning the show for months, since she had become housebound after Thanksgiving of last year.

I'm a Legend!

Who's buying?

We made a list of the ones we knew were still alive, tracked down a few more we hadn't heard from in eons. (Did you know that Chanelle Tempest was now managing a trailer park in the Everglades? How the Gorgeous Ones have fallen, Honey Child!) Miss Sincerely Peaches made up a list of the great performances she would like to see done when the time should arrive for them to be done and she had saved a puddle of cash since Day One, and since her longtime Mr. You Know Who had been a long-standing member of the Peachtree Driving Club, there was never a question of where we were going to do it (and that stiff-and-stuffy ole place needed a good airing out, if you want my truthful opinion, no matter how much they continue to defend and promote their new "openness" and "good citizenship" toward our community).

Of course there were no decent dressing rooms (just like the old days) and the ladies raised a bit of a ruckus about tucking behind a curtain. And yes, there were some complaints about the order of the evening—when Hot Coco got wind that she was going on after Marsha Mella she

had a hissy fit and there was no chance
for a few of the out-of-towners like
Sabrina Flair to rehearse the room. (Yes,
yes, yes, even Miss Tanya Hyde worked her
sorry, leathery ass up from Miami and
Tiffany Blue and Creatta Blaze drove in
from New Orleans for this truly fabulous
gathering of sisters, which should have been
videotaped for posterity's sake.)

   Moi opened the show with my
best number from Charity ———
"I'm a Brass Band" —— (and I
still fit into that spangled-
feathery mess of a costume, too,
Mary Sue, I want you to know)—→
and then served as the Mistress
of Insufferable Ceremonies, as I
often did back in our old
Legacy evenings. Peaches had even
scripted some things I could
say about the sisters who
returned for the Celebration, like
reminding Trashetta that she was always
out of style, but there were plenty of
divine and inspired impromptu diva moments,
like Raven MacQueen talking about how
her parents thought for 25 years she was
teaching dance on Cheshire Bridge (and
Mary Belle, let me remind you, she did

teach a lot of people a certain kind of movement.), and of course Missy Manchester got up and told that same sorry story about the night she won Miss Gay America at the Glass Menagerie and how she was lifted into superstardom and all of us—and I do mean all of us—rolled our eyes in disgust and dismay at having to Witness Again to that Same Tired Thang. The best moment of the night, however, belonged to Mercédes Porsche, who reminded us that back in the Olden Days when she was working at the Chances R Lounge in Birmingham, she had to wear at least 3 pieces of men's clothing when she sang, otherwise her sorry ass could be whisked off to jail (which made me believe, truly believe, sweet Mary Jane, that she was indeed older than Peaches).

Yes, dearest Billy Boy, you missed the tears and cheers. Ray La Ray made me absolutely certain that I was watching Cher sing and Hot Coco emerged from that gorilla suit in her best platinum—blonde do and sang "Better Get Ready for Love," surrounded by a puddle of young thangs wearing only their stomach muscles and

Leopard Loincloths, which raised my frail and feeble pulse to a truly dangerous level!

(And yes, Sweetie Pie, there were some notable no-shows besides your beautiful ass, most importantly that sorry-mouthed Holly divine, who could not work it up to fly in from Germany, where she has now proclaimed herself Royalty — and after all that Peaches did for her—and I do mean everything!!)

I'm a real queen!

Afterward, a few of us drank and sang around that lovely white baby grand in the divine ballroom that overlooks the 18th hole (or 18th whore, as Peaches always liked to moan). By then Sabrina had left, so the rest of us were free to trash her. She has started to look down on The Ones Who Lip Synch because she considered herself The Real Thing now that she sings every single wrong and messy lyric with her hoary and raspy off-key voice. Rumor has it, Sweetie, that Sabrina has had more than the recent nip and tuck done to her eyes. Coco, in fact, said that there was nothing real at all left to her—she was a fake from head to toe—and of course she asked, Why, Oh Why, Did Peaches Feel She Had to Invite

I've got a secret too!

that One Back? It was up to me to defend
Peaches, which I had to do without spilling
all the beans about the sordid past between
those two girls.

But soon we had
left that miserable subject
behind and were talking about all those
colossal beauties and gorgeous boys who
worked or started out at The Legacy and it
was Mercedes, dearest, who said that You
had become a truly gifted writer, even if
you were drawn to all that was Divine and
Glum about Our Galaxy. Trashetta said
that she could not finish your latest Opus
about the last moments of those two
dying men because a certain passage had
provoked a crying jag that she did not
intend to revisit, and I told them all about
the time Peaches and I went to the downtown
library and found you indexed in the card
catalog. (We squealed so much, Honey Bee,
that we were asked to leave by a
Sourpuss Friend of Dorothy, who sneered
and wanted nothing to do with us More
Beautiful Ones.) Even on her death bed
Peaches remarked how proud she was that
you had become A Most Momentous Writer
because of all the Important Things You

were writing about, though she
let out a tiny wish and a
big-assed =Sigh= that you
would write something fanciful
about your young and lively
times at Lady Belle's Legacy.
(Not to mention the hotter times
across the street at the Locker
Room). I reminded her that
perhaps it was best that You
not recall ALL of those days
that could only spell trouble for The
Rest of Us, because not only were they
lively, they were also deadly for some,
and I ain't referring to That Virus We
Knew Nothing About In Those Days.

And this is the true reason why I
am writing you, my darling Sweet Little
Sister. Peaches did not carry her secrets
to the grave—she gave away her beauty
tips to whomever would show up to her
suite in the final days, but the most
horrible fact was that on a few occasions
she let that swarthy and foreign-born
Skeleton out of her closet, if you catch
my drift. Not that it mattered, really,

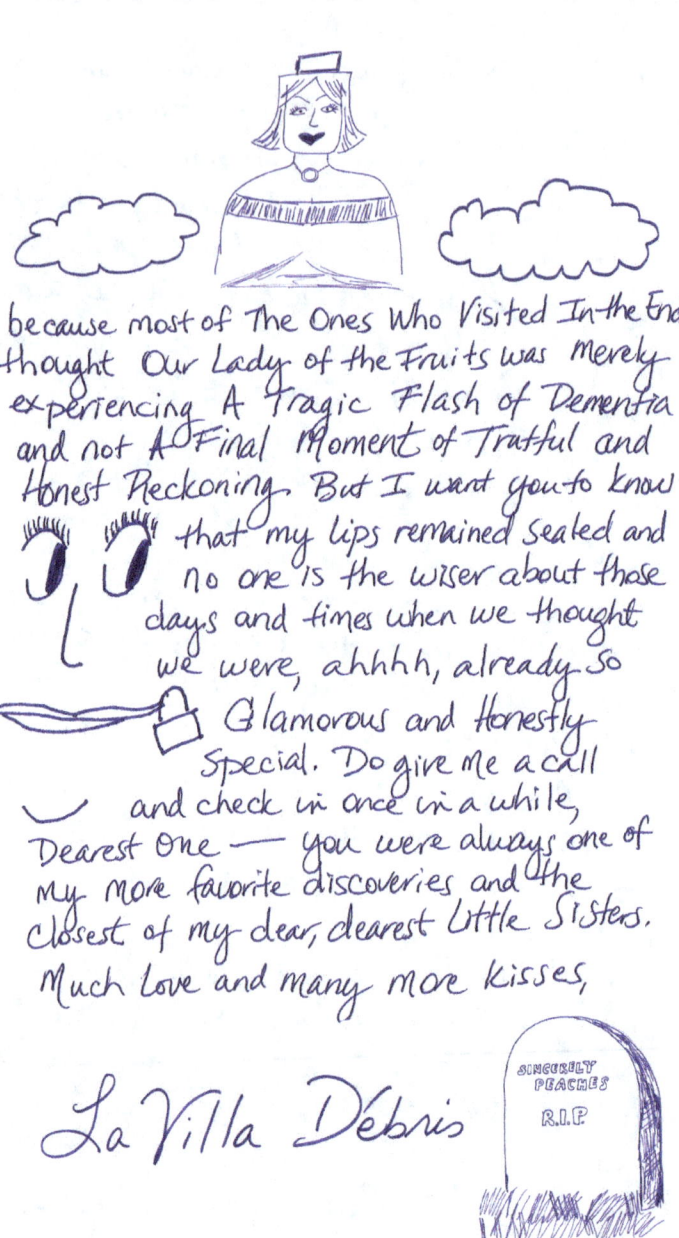

because most of The Ones Who Visited In the End
thought Our Lady of the Fruits was merely
experiencing A Tragic Flash of Dementia
and not A Final Moment of Truthful and
Honest Reckoning. But I want you to know
that my lips remained sealed and
no one is the wiser about those
days and times when we thought
we were, ahhhh, already so
Glamorous and Honestly
Special. Do give me a call
and check in once in a while,
Dearest One — you were always one of
my more favorite discoveries and the
closest of my dear, dearest Little Sisters.
Much Love and many more kisses,

La Villa Débris

SINCERELY
PEACHES
R.I.P.

The following story was originally published in *The Village Quorum*, Vol. 21, Issue 4, dated Winter 2000, and is reprinted courtesy of the Goodman Foundation and the Estate of William B. Goodman.

Illustrations by Sean Burke and used with permission of the artist.

THE MAN THAT GOT AWAY

William B. Goodman

I've avoided telling this story for a number of reasons. Foremost, I think, is that I find myself having been so young when these events occurred; I was eighteen that year and a sophomore in college, still naïve about the world around me and how I might be perceived by others. Who I was then seems so foreign to me—cynical, jaded, and over-experienced as I now am—and I am concerned that I am unable to accurately recapture the feelings of those times, and the events may seem clichéd and the characters stereotypical because of the overlapping prisms of history, culture, and my own youthful impressions. And it is a difficult story to tell. If I were to write up front that this story is about a murder and its characters are drag queens and a drug dealer, I doubt that I would be able to gather much respect or compassion from a reader about the subtle truths of what happened to me and my friends and the depth of its reverberation in our lives. And it doesn't help that I am ashamed of some of my own actions, particularly in the cover-up of the crime and my fleeing to escape my guilt. I am also hard-pressed to say that there was a love-affair gone wrong—or, rather, several gone bad. Nonetheless, I will plow ahead because I want to set the record... *straight,* as it were, given that many of the players are unfortunately no longer around due to an unforeseen virus that reimagined the landscape before we could do it ourselves.

Those days were both fearless and full of fear—it was the fall of 1974, the country was still reeling from the shock

Billy Goodman

of the Watergate scandal and the resignation of President Nixon. Eighteen was a legal drinking age in the State of Georgia. It was five years after the Stonewall Riots, though that was a historical event I knew nothing about at the time because that sort of news did not travel as openly as it does now—this story begins in a queer old South that was ready for change but had not yet changed. To be gay in those days in Atlanta meant keeping the fact secret almost all the time, or at least during the daylight hours, waiting for nightfall to arrive, when you could come alive as your true self at one of the clubs on Cheshire Bridge Road, just south of Lindbergh. These were usually reached through rear entrances of small industrial-looking buildings whose unmarked doors led to discos or drag bars or bathhouses and dark, smoky rooms punctured by twirling, spinning colored lights and irresistible, pounding music. Walking through those doors was a little bit like walking into Oz, a destination of heady, giddy exuberance for those who wanted to be there. I remember the fluttery heartbeat I felt when I stepped inside Magic Garden or the Locker Room or Hollywood Hots or Lady Belle's Legacy or the Sweet Gum Head, ready to see who was at the bar and who was ready to dance and who was about to prance up on stage and perform. In those days, I needed something or someone exciting to convince me that I had made the right choice in what I was doing and who I was becoming. To quote one of the drag queens I knew at this time—he went by the name of LaVilla Débris, "If you don't visit Parée, Honey Child, how you gonna know you've left the farm?"

Which is not far from the truth in my case. I didn't exactly grow up on a farm, but I did grow up in a small Southern town, small in both its narrow religious view and the size of its population, and which sheltered and isolated me as if I *were* growing up on a farm. Our house bordered a lake and large tracts of forested slopes and small mountains. The nearest neighbor was three miles away. My childhood was one of Bible camps and little league baseball teams; in high school I was socially a loner, trapped in a middle ground between the popular kids and the rednecks. I was not sharp, witty, or a jokester; more of the guy always overlooked in the hallway because there was always someone more cool or dangerous standing in front or behind me. I wasn't any good at math or science—Chemistry frightened me and Geometry left me confused, but I did well in History because I was good at remembering facts. I'd left home to attend college in the northern part of the state, a mistake I realized soon thereafter, because I had, in fact, enrolled in a college that specialized in agriculture, even though I knew I had no desire to be a farmer. The campus was full of rolling green hills, wide, deep ponds, and bordered by large bucolic tracts of corn and grain, and I quickly learned that such a pastoral pace was too slow for me. My awakening arrived the spring of my freshman year when I took a course in literature of the 1920s and read novels and stories and memoirs of fast times in Paris, London, and New York, often while I was alone, sitting on a bench far from the other students out by a pond near the edges of the campus I had grown to love. It was an ironic discovery—encountering city lives so full of vibrancy while trapped in rustic, academic isolation. I loved the physical beauty of that campus but I also felt like I was missing out on something that should define me as who I was meant to be. I knew I had to change my course. My sophomore year I transferred to a university in Atlanta where the tuition was more expensive, the buildings more urban, and the state of mind was more cosmopolitan.

I'd only made up my mind to change schools at the last possible minute, so I'd missed the application deadline and been shut out of the dormitories. Well, I didn't really miss it, if the truth be told, and I am trying to tell the truth here—I was unable to make the deadline because my college education was on my own dime, my father's income being no more than a poor farmer's; our family of six had subsisted on his wages as a factory technician at a food processing plant and my mother's earnings as an elementary schoolteacher, which explained why I had originally chosen the school in the bucolic Blue Ridge mountains that had offered me a scholarship. I didn't have enough money to write a check to accompany the dormitory residence application, so instead, I found a less expensive alternative, a week-to-week room off-campus in a house owned by an elderly woman who lived with a fiercely yapping chihuahua named Rodney, a tiny monster who seemed to be perpetually in heat, ready to hump my leg in the kitchen the moment I stood still. This unpleasant housing arrangement left me shut out of the kind of urban, communal collegiate experience I had so desired when I decided to change schools and now, entering my second year of college, I again found myself alone and too shy to reach out to my new classmates, all of whom seemed more urban and hip and "with it" than I was.

Those first few weeks I tried to uncover ways of finding friends or someone to talk to—at the library, at the cafeteria, at the midnight film screenings in the basement of the campus student center—all without much luck. One guy tried to convince me to go through pledge week—but I knew I wasn't the fraternity sort of guy—and then the weeks passed and I was soon overwhelmed by study and work— to make ends meet, or, rather, to *try* to make ends meet, I worked part-time at a twenty-four-hour grocery store near campus, bagging purchases and restocking merchandise. And then one day I found myself staring at the bulletin board at the university student center, reading a flyer about auditions for a campus theatrical group that was doing a production of the stage musical, *Hello, Dolly!*

I was familiar with the title song of the show, having heard it on the radio a zillion times when I was growing up. I had bought the original cast album and then later the soundtrack to the movie, after I had seen the film on one of the few dates I had subjected myself to in high school— with Amy Birch, a more popular girl a year younger than myself—and I had enjoyed watching the movie more than being with Amy. I had no musical comedy gifts except for my love and appreciation of movies and dancing and theater and music. When I was a boy of seven or eight, my father had made the tragic mistake of taking me to see a touring production of *The Unsinkable Molly Brown!* that starred a well-known television star. It had been a big event for our family—dressing up in our Sunday clothes and driving into the big city to see a live stage show under a starry night sky at the outdoor amphitheater at Chastain Park—and by the time we had returned home later that night and I was alone in my bedroom, I was practicing my routines in front of the mirror, singing "Belly Up to the Bar Boys," and high-kicking until I would lose my balance and tumble to the floor in giggles. I suppose that indicates a cliché about myself or who I was on the road to becoming, but the truth was that I had no performing talents. I could not sing on key or move my feet with any kind of rhythm no matter how many new musicals and composers and performers I discovered. And my miserable high school date only emphasized that I had developed few social skills—a very limited range unable to engage others or keep myself from being miserable in their presence. All I had by the time I was a sophomore in college was the "right look" to be on stage—desire coupled with a simple boyish attractiveness.

I had not prepared anything to sing or recite when I showed up at the campus auditions for *Hello, Dolly!*—I knew my limitations even though I was prepared to ignore them. I thought that I might volunteer to help backstage or paint sets or find the right props, though I secretly hoped that instead I might be discovered as "just the right kind of guy we were hoping to find for that starring role." I was asked by the director, a balding law student, to sing an a cappella version of "The Star-Spangled Banner," which I awkwardly struggled through, and then told to check the bulletin board in a couple of days to see if I had made the cast. For a while I thought that because I had been cast in the chorus the balding law student must have thought I had displayed some kind of promising talent, but sometime during the second week of rehearsals, I overheard another cast member say that the director had desperately cast anyone who had showed up for auditions. This was about the same time the pre-law and pre-med students began dropping out of the cast because they were worried about their grades and I was added to the group of guys who were to be the waiters at the Harmonia Gardens, an expensive, highfalutin restaurant in New York City that Dolly Levi visits in the musical, a number that our law school director intended to be an elaborate spectacle of entrances and exits and athletic theatrics.

The part of the Head Waiter was being played by a fellow named David Duffy, an alumnus of the university who had stringy long hair. He was in his late twenties and worked as a teller at a nearby bank—some cast members had seen him there or in one of the other campus shows he had done before I had enrolled at the university. David displayed a

David Duffy
aka
LaVilla Débris

towering confidence on stage. He was tall and lanky with a face that resembled putty, and by that I mean he could stretch his mouth and widen his already oversized lips and eyes and eyebrows into the most outrageous expressions, as if he were a French mime auditioning to replace Lucille Ball in her sitcom. I found him quite fascinating to watch because he could flash through an entire spectrum of emotions within seconds, at a time when I was struggling to understand many of my own. David had a high-toned, fluty, snooty voice that added to his comic appeal and made it unnecessary for anyone else to share the stage with him. David, however, soon realized that his stage presence was made more comical by the bland and inexperienced accompaniment of the rest of us, especially when he discovered during rehearsals that not only could I *not* do a cartwheel or a backflip, but I could not even carry a tray or walk across the stage in time to the beat of the music. His impromptu "bit"—to stop and start me until I got it right— made everyone at rehearsals laugh, while I turned unnatural shades of red in embarrassment and frustration. I was close to quitting at that moment, though something in my gut told me to bear it up and stick it out.

David was also something of a mother hen to the other cast members and a good friend of the balding director—I had noticed him at many rehearsals engaged in what looked like serious and private discussions with other cast members, usually one of the girls in the chorus, drawing them to his chest, patting their hair as they sobbed to him about something, then grasping them seriously by the shoulders and looking them straight in the eyes. I had no such drama to confide to David and often thought of myself only as an observer, not as someone being observed, certainly not as a performer attempting to command the attention of an audience. David also made a point to interrupt Neal, our director, to explain why the choreography was looking so sloppy in one scene or another, and we would have to start the scene or song over again, or decompose it step by step or word by word and practice, practice, practice, with David embarrassing others as he had done initially to me. One night after rehearsals were over, David took me aside and walked me through every step I was supposed to make during the title number of the show. He corrected my posture and gave me a speed course in military training. "Being a waiter is a lot like being a private in the Army," he said. "You're a robotic fool only following orders. Break character and you could land in the slammer." I was both flattered and intimidated that I was the close focus of someone's attention, and I practiced my steps over and over, trying to make both him and myself proud. David had convinced a shaggy blond fellow named Austin, who played the piano at rehearsals, to remain behind with us that evening and pound out the beats as I learned my routine. While I learned to balance a silver tray on my upturned palm, the two of them lobbed questions at me as though they were trying out a new set of musical comedy skills: Where did I live? What was I studying? Where had I grown up? Who, in fact, were my people?

"My people?" I asked, stopping my walking.

"Are you a good witch or a bad witch?" David asked.

When I didn't immediately respond, he added, "Husband or hustler?"

I still didn't know how to answer him and he proceeded ahead without me. "Husband, of course," he said. "Your hesitation clearly shows that. Harriett Key Bored over there just wanted to make sure." He nodded in the direction of Austin.

The context of these remarks flew over my head. I had no understanding then of camp names and gay slang or sexual innuendo or that such codes and clues even existed. In fact, I didn't even know that David was gay because I didn't know that I was gay myself, or, rather, I hadn't acknowledged and accepted the fact that I was gay, though it was clear to others around me, particularly those gay men in the cast, that I was a show tune waiting to be belted out. I didn't know that Austin had confessed an interest in me to David, which was the real reason why he was there to help me learn my beats. Austin didn't put any moves on me that night, nor did David, but there was plenty of speculation about the sexuality of everyone in the cast—the girls in the chorus were interested in any of the guys the guys weren't already interested in, and, as soon as word got around that Austin had *not* put the moves on me at that after-rehearsal rehearsal, a chesty girl named Nancy Greenberger thrust *her* interest upon me. She came on strong, wanting to know where I was living, what I was studying, what kind of sports I was interested in. I was soon dodging her suggestions for sharing a pizza by going back to the dormitories with a guy named Cliff Jackson, another fellow who had been cast as one of the dancing and singing waiters. Cliff came from the same kind of small town, small-minded, too-religious Southern family as my own, but he could carry a tune and do cartwheels and handstands, which made him a popular choice for both the guys and the girls in the cast and made me feel lucky to have him want to spend time with me. Cliff had had a series of high school girlfriends he referred to as "unpromising" and "restrictive," and like myself, he had successfully eluded the traps of bosomy, man-hungry Nancy Greenberger, and this gave us something shared to laugh about. Cliff also knew who was gay in the cast and

Cliff Jackson

who was not, though in those early days of our getting to know each other he neglected to label or identify any of his own feelings. He was the one who told me the reason behind Austin's arranging my extra rehearsal—Austin had wanted to know me "better." I didn't know whether to be upset or flattered and looked to Cliff for clues on how I should accept or react to this news.

"He's incredibly talented," Cliff said, dropping the gay subject and moving beyond revealing any "personal dirt" about Austin. "He's written some songs and had one recorded."

"Is it on the radio?"

"I only heard a demo. It's a dance song. David loves it."

Cliff's subtle references also washed by me—the fact that he had heard Austin's demo song somewhere, that it was something to dance to in the clubs, and that Cliff was more friendly with David than I was aware of. But Cliff loved sharing his love of music and musicals with me. In Cliff's dorm room we studied and listened to music—he had an eclectic array of albums, from Chuck Mangione's *World of Make Believe* to the original cast album of *You're a Good Man, Charlie Brown*. Cliff and I were the same height, which was why we had been paired together in the waiter's dancing routine, though his physique had been sharpened by a high school with a strong gymnastics program. He had deep brown eyes, dark, spiky hair naturally lightened by being out in the sun, and a wide jaw that made him handsome. He also had an intense drive to keep himself entertained, which usually meant dipping into his supply of marijuana, replenished by a never-seen older brother who lived in Buckhead. The first time I smoked a joint in Cliff's dorm room I was paranoid about being caught in the act by the powers that be, whomever or whatever They were, and was worried about the repercussions that might follow, however dire and horrendous Those could be, from expulsion from college to losing my part-time job to growing breasts and becoming a deadhead, unable to speak or think or, gasp, even walk across the stage in an amateur musical comedy production. I was unable to articulate this, of course, or only communicate it in rambling nonsensical word patterns that Cliff seemed to instinctively understand. Cliff had no such paranoia. He showed me how to act cool and unfazed while I was stoned, as well as demonstrating while we were high how to focus on a musical phrase that was repeated in a recorded song—a trumpet trill or a guitar riff, for instance. As my eyes dilated and my breathing calmed, the notes soared out of the speakers and sparkled in the air and the words in my textbooks walked off the pages and assembled into bold-lettered marquees of Absolutely Great Thoughts or Completely Unnecessary Things. It was a Totally New and Exciting Time for me.

"Play the key change again," I would ask and Cliff would jump up from his chair and replace the needle on the record where a song modulated up to an upper chord. I loved watching him move through the tiny space of his dorm room, an elegant gazelle leaping over a pile of books and clothes and shoes towards his stereo console, and Cliff loved playing the older, wiser brother illuminating life to his less experienced charge. I often think of him as the first true friend I ever had—someone who enjoyed my company as much as I enjoyed his.

"It's the same song, but different," Cliff would add and I would watch him dip the stereo handle to the vinyl record, his hand shaking because of his eagerness. "It just builds and builds higher and higher till it has nowhere to go but to stop," he said, his voice rising higher and louder with excitement.

I had a great awe of Cliff, larger, even, than the one I had of David, in part, because I found Cliff more physically attractive, though I could not openly state that fact or even acknowledge it. One night while he was dipping into his stash Cliff confided to me that he'd "been" with several guys, and I could not prevent my astonishment from registering on my face because I had never before had a close friend who had revealed anything intimate like this, certainly not one who was gay. But I didn't know if I was the same or different from Cliff—I had developed no real sexual fantasies of guys or girls—I masturbated for the intense pleasure it provided me, the ability it gave me to focus on only the thing in my hand and how it felt when I held and stroked it and reached an orgasm, not because I was imagining there was another person with me. One night, Cliff and I were both sitting on the floor, our backs against the frame of his bed, his roommate long since banished to some other place. We were listening to a Bee Gees album and smoking and attempting to study but talking about this or that as impromptu thoughts roamed through our minds. At one moment, when my eyes lifted away from the textbook I had thought I was reading and drifted toward Cliff, Cliff's eyes met mine and he leaned in to kiss me.

This is not a story about coming out, though it did happen that I did so at this time and it is something I must write through in order to get to the other events and truths of this story. That night Cliff's kiss had so shaken me that I had leapt up and left him alone in his dorm room, embarrassed, confused, and thrilled by it all. I had never kissed a guy before. In fact, my deepest experience with a woman thus far (a girl, really) had been limited to a high school classmate who chased me and then complained that I was unresponsive to her needs. It had never bothered me that I had not found a girlfriend or that I was a "virgin" in the technical definition of having sex with another person, but it worried me that this could be due to a deep attraction toward men—or at least toward Cliff. But I was also worried that if I was not gay, or unable to accept it or to respond to Cliff, it might mean losing his friendship.

The next time I saw Cliff was two days later at rehearsal. I didn't know how to react, so I kept to myself, sitting on the floor of a hallway outside the rehearsal room reading my Ancient Civilizations book until our scene was called. I was deeply troubled because I did not want Cliff to dislike me because I had rebuffed him. And I didn't understand my own feelings of what I was experiencing. The director was rehearsing the actors playing Dolly and Vandergelder—something was not to his liking—and he soon dismissed the rest of the cast for the night so he could work alone with the actress playing Dolly. As the news was passed down the hallway from person to person, Cliff arrived where I was sitting and said, "Still friends?"

"Of course," I answered, then lied about having a history exam that I had to study for. The shame from my lie flushed across my face and I said next, in a rather hurried way, "I'm confused."

"Yeah, I hate history, too," Cliff answered.

I couldn't find words to better explain myself, and I was lucky that Cliff had understood—or misunderstood—my comment, and I asked him, "How did you know?"

I saw his posture change, from the relief of our easy reconciliation to something that required more of his attention and concern. He slid down the wall to sit beside me on the floor. "I always knew," he said, slowly, whispering so that his voice would not travel. "It was always there. Whenever I was reading a book. Or watching TV. That I wanted to know the guy, not the girl. That's how I knew it wasn't wrong. It wasn't a sin. It was always the natural way for me to feel even when everyone said the opposite. It's not a punishment from God. If anything, it's a challenge."

The opportunity for another kiss did not happen that night, or the next because I had to skip rehearsals to work a double shift at the grocery store, but after the next rehearsal Cliff mentioned that there was a group of cast members going dancing at a club off-campus and asked if I wanted to join them. The others included two girls, one of whom was the man-hungry, chesty Nancy Greenberger, and I felt they had approached me to join them because I had a car and I could drive everyone to the club. It feels odd to me to write now that up to then I had never been out dancing with friends or been to a disco or a nightclub, when it seems like such a natural thing for a young man to have already experienced, but as I have already tried to explain, my social orbit was a limited one. And I had moved to Atlanta to be included in moments like this—so how could I think about refusing to join them, even if I thought they were only using me to get to the place they wanted to go?

I was not aware that it was a gay nightclub until we had parked our cars and reached an unmarked door at the back of a building that appeared to be empty. "This is a club?" I asked Cliff. There was no neon sign, no ticket booth, no awning above the door to make it look distinct.

"You're not scared?" Cliff asked.

I didn't understand the substance behind his question, which immediately made me nervous and scared, but Nancy and her friend Cindy had already made it to the door, which opened up to a narrow hallway where there was a man seated before a card table where a metal cash box was placed. We each paid a few dollars for admission, had the back of our hands stamped with an ink imprint that I would later discover glowed beneath ultraviolet light, and entered a larger room where there was a bar against one of the walls. My memory recreates that club as cavernous and electric, even though a return visit many years later would reveal it to be much smaller—there was a neon rainbow hanging near the top of a wall; at the ceiling was a crisscross of spot lights that blinked with different colors and a mirror-covered ball in the center that lowered and spun and sent twirling rays of light around the darkened room. The music was deafening—a heavy, thumping bass that I am surprised that I don't recall hearing as we approached the building, but I suppose my excitement and fear had washed it away. Cliff grabbed my hand and led me through the crowd to the dance floor. It was odd to hold a guy's hand, as large and rough as my own, to feel him pulling me through and around other dancing couples, a sensation of both pleasure and confusion. He stopped at a point near the center of the room and started dancing and it was only then that I realized he wanted me to dance with him and that we were in a gay club. He smiled at me and I watched him mouth "loosen up."

I must have remained in place, unable to budge because I had realized how stiff and nervous I was, because Cliff stepped closer, slid his hands around my waist, and began moving his hips back and forth, nodding for me to mirror him. There was a thrilling consciousness to the fact that he was so close to me, to see the minute details of his face and skin and eyes, but even more to know that there was someone so interested in my mood and opinion and welfare. I still didn't know who I was at this moment, only that I wanted to see if the person I should be was the one who was here with Cliff. I must have reddened and looked around, thinking someone was watching us, but no one was—we were in a shadowy room of men dancing, shifting, smiling, stepping to the beat. Nancy and Cindy were nowhere to be seen. There were, in fact, no women within my view. When I looked back to Cliff he kissed me briefly to comfort and reassure me and pulled back to gauge my reaction. I rocked my hips back and forth, feeling awkward to have Cliff's hands placed against the small of my back, and he smiled and pressed his forehead against mine as we lightly danced together. I know I made the next move because I remember it as a momentous one, even though it was only a small physical shift of my body. I tilted my head so it was at an angle to Cliff's and leaned into him and kissed him.

I count this as one my unforgettable memories—the closeness in the dark, the dancing, the thumping music, the spinning lights, my own confusion and delight. The only time we stopped dancing was to get a drink. When Nancy and Cindy found us later, ready to go back to campus, our shirts and jeans were soaked with sweat, and I was smiling like I had never done so before.

I dropped the girls off at their dormitory, then drove Cliff to his. It was late October, Halloween was a few days away, and I was wildly awake. I could smell the change of the weather in the leaves and the soil as I pulled to a stop in front of Cliff's dorm, hoping that we might kiss some more.

"You can park over there," he pointed to a lot. I hadn't expected anything to go further than the kiss—I thought Cliff's roommate would be an obstacle, but Cliff said, "Jeff's away. He took his girlfriend to Chattanooga for the weekend."

I parked the car and we bounded up the stairs to his room, laughing at ourselves and our speed—there were others on his hall that were still up—doors were open revealing dark rooms and crazy colored lights—lava lamps and paper lanterns and shadowy figures of guys reclining on their beds smoking dope and listening to music that spilled out into the bright hall as we passed them.

When we reached Cliff's room, I followed him inside, but unlike other times I had spent with him there he did not flip on the overhead light. He stood in the dark and pulled the wet T-shirt over his head and paused in the light that filtered into the room from the campus streetlights. I found it mesmerizing, the way the light caressed the side of his neck and shoulder. I wanted to always be with him, to never leave him, to always have him guiding me someplace new. I wanted to be inside his skin, to know what he knew, to laugh and smile at all the things he laughed and smiled at. He unbuttoned his jeans and slipped out of them and I saw the heft of his cock in his underwear.

When he turned to throw the shirt and jeans onto a chair I began unbuttoning my shirt, feeling the cool air hit my skin as I pulled the wet fabric away. I could feel myself smiling and shaking with excitement. When I was undressed, Cliff stepped in front of me as he had at the club, only now his hands ran along my skin. My hands ran along the sides of his body and our faces floated into another kiss. We kissed for a long time, standing, pressed tightly together, then he pulled away, and I felt the spring at our groins. He took a hand and reached down and cupped and squeezed, testing my reaction to his deliberate action. I smiled at the pleasure of it, the pleasure of being with him, and I could feel the breath from his mouth brushing against my own as I reached for him.

I won't linger over more details—that's not my intent here—though there were hours of this sort of physical attention demonstrated to one another—I only want to reveal the deep set of emotions that had come tumbling out of me whenever I was with Cliff—that night, other nights, and the rest of the time I knew him.

I stayed with Cliff until the morning, when I had to leave to work a shift at the store. I remember the despair I felt as I left him in his narrow bed and showered alone in the restroom at the dormitory, redressing in the musky clothes I had worn the night before.

But we began a routine of finding each other every day—for lunch, for studying, for sex. We would walk across campus together—to his class or mine, to the library, to rehearsals, to his dorm or even to house where I rented a room, a respite where we could laugh, smoke, undress and caress each other without the worry of discovery. His mood was always buoyant and euphoric. Our bodies fit perfectly together spooning or embracing. We would lie together, talking or listening to music: Bette Midler, Manhattan Transfer, a cast album I had discovered at the record store. My elderly landlady was often napping or deeply asleep, so our noisemaking never disturbed her, and even the ever-barking Rodney embraced Cliff—he would bark at our arrival, now a notice of greeting to Cliff and a growl of annoyance at me—and then he would do a silent happy dance and quietly disappear to his favorite pillow.

I'd been bitten by the theater bug as strongly as the love one. I had discovered *The Matchmaker*, the play that had inspired *Hello, Dolly!*, and learned that it had been inspired by a French farce, and I had spent long hours at the university library sifting through text books about the theater, sitting at a carrel reading about commedia dell'arte. In the bedroom, I asked about Cliff's theatrical experiences: his favorite roles, his favorite songs, his favorite composers. He'd been in *The Sound of Music* (as Rolf), *Oliver!* (as an orphan), and *A Funny Thing Happened on the Way to the Forum* (as Hero).

"A funny thing happened to me in that show," he confessed to me one night.

"What was that?"

"I let Miles Glorious give me a blow job."

"Who was that?"

"A character in the play. In *Forum*."

I gave him an astonished look, and he clarified with a laugh, "Not during the play. *Backstage*."

I offered a wide smile because I was learning about this myself—the methods of sex between men. Our heads were side by side then on the pillows and I recall how lucky I felt to be with sòmeone like Cliff. Years later when I came across a discussion of Plato's theory about an incomplete soul yearning for its other half, I thought I was reading about myself and Cliff.

But I can't say that even then, at that moment, I identified as gay. I thought of myself as a young man with Cliff. I thought of us as boyfriends, a couple, partners. I had no desire to date anyone else or look for another sex partner. I was happy and content. No, I was more than that. I was in love. And it was first love, the one that is the hardest to shake. Cliff, I learned, had never had a boyfriend before—he'd never "dated" a guy, never slept with the same guy more than twice, and had never been in a relationship. He was patient about everything I didn't understand and I never failed to notice the joy in his step when we were together.

Of course I am aware now of the small, closed universe my happiness was contained in. But even so, it wasn't without difficulty. There were little digs from Cliff over how much cologne I was wearing or if I was using too many hand gestures while talking or if I were dressed "too gay" or "too inappropriately" to be seen together. In many respects, I owe my desire for subtlety to those gentle put-downs from Cliff. I learned how to be conspicuous in the gay world and invisible in the straight one, how to discern the secret "gay signals" coming at me from strangers while at the grocery store or the library, and how to shift gears in an instant when I was uncertain of another man's sexuality, though I would never master the techniques of "cruising." There was also a delicate balancing act of how we identified ourselves and how we acted together around others—we had no roadmap, no role models, no study guides or lists of dos and don'ts. I disliked being labeled gay—the term seemed incorrect to me—and Cliff disliked being called boyfriends—because it seemed inappropriate to how he felt. We settled on being referred to as "best friends," which worked with those who knew our deeper feelings for each other and those who didn't, though our fellow cast members would often refer to us as a unit: "CliffandBilly" or "BillyandCliff" because we were always together.

The performances of *Hello, Dolly!* were a hit on campus. My Southern Lit professor stopped me on campus one day to commend me on my dancing skills in the waiter's number. New experiences continued, but they often arrived with a steep learning curve attached. We went dancing again at Backstreet, the gay club in midtown, with Nancy and Cindy to midnight showings of *Pink Flamingos*, a John Waters film starring a drag queen named Divine, and then with Austin to see David perform at Lady Belle's Legacy, another gay club on Cheshire Bridge Road. David, I discovered, was more than a part-time bank teller and our officious *Hello, Dolly!* cast mate and choreographer. He was female impersonator named LaVilla Débris, a guy who dressed up in women's clothing and told off-color jokes. He also mouthed the lyrics of songs sung by famous female vocalists that blasted out of giant stereo speakers.

I had never seen a live drag show before and found it enjoyable, but baffling. "Why would a guy want to wear a dress?" I asked Cliff.

"To create an illusion," Austin said. "Of being a woman."

"Why would a man want to be a woman?"

They both laughed at me. "It's a performance," Cliff added. "Like *Pink Flamingos*."

"David likes being more outrageous than pretty," Austin explained.

"But he's already funny," I said. "Why does he need to wear a dress?"

Understanding gay culture doesn't happen because you desire another guy. The humor, lingo, and secret codes don't simply arrive along with the physical and emotional connection. I had to have the definition of what was "camp" explained to me more than once and I could never understand why every gay man was referred to as "Mary." Double-entendres usually washed over me. To this day, I still struggle with how gay a gay man should be and if I am gay enough to be considered as "gay" as others.

I mention this because it wasn't like I was suddenly sexually liberated, culturally shrewd, *and* politically liberal. I also struggled with my faith and religion, with the laws and regulations of the state and city I lived in, with the shame and guilt and dangers that society and history had linked with being homosexual. I worried at every step that I was doing something wrong, that someone would denounce me. But that did not prevent me from doing what seemed right and natural to me and continuing on the path I had chosen for myself—to continue seeing Cliff, to meet up with him, to know him, to love him, to experience him.

Thanksgiving break rolled around and I found myself at home, pinning away for Cliff, unable to express to my family what I was feeling for him. I was the third of four children, adept at living in the shadows of my older siblings, and I never expected or wanted my parents to uncover any of my new "misbehavior," which would be how they would view it. My family was focused on maintaining a good-standing and reputation in our community and our community was defined to our church, where we had been members for many years. My sister had been a cheerleader and had married her high school boyfriend days after her graduation, and her new child, Jesse, my nephew, had recently been baptized. My older brother had been an Eagle Scout and I had never been able to live up to his reputation, so it was easier to accept that I was different from him and other guys and that there was nothing wrong in being so. My Thanksgiving was spent feeling ungrateful because I had to keep my new life hidden. I was thankful, in fact, that I could not spend too much time with them; I was needed in Atlanta to cover shifts for co-workers at the store who wanted to spend *more* time with their families.

When Cliff returned to Atlanta from the holiday break I felt he had changed. Something had made him different—or different with me, an aloofness had crept into his attitude when we were together. He was vague about spending time with me—there were reasons why he needed time alone, to be on his own, and I didn't know if the root of this was the truth or an excuse. Cliff had spent the holiday with his family as well, and I wondered if the sort of guilt that had plagued me was also troubling him—if somehow he had had a change of heart and he was not gay anymore, if he now thought of himself as a sinner who needed to repent and change his ways, that in the eyes of God and in the word of the Bible what we were doing together was not right, even if it seemed utterly natural to both of us. But he explained that the break from classes had made him fall behind in his courses and he needed time alone to concentrate. He found me too distracting. Cliff was a more determined student than I was, but he didn't have to work a part-time job to pay for his tuition; all he had was time to study, so his newfound reticence to spend time with me bothered me, even though final exams were approaching. I had never considered Cliff a distraction—he had always been a companion—and he had never been a deterrent from my own studies.

"What's wrong?" I asked him one afternoon when I found him in the cafeteria. We had not gotten together since we had both returned from the holiday break—I had called him several nights at his dorm and asked him to come over to the house, but the excuses had continued.

"Nothing," he answered, and I knew that was a lie. I could sense that he was giving up on us, or giving up on me. Something had changed his mind, and I wanted to know what it was. I wasn't ready to give up on him.

"Why are you avoiding me?" I asked him.

"We're becoming too serious," he answered, then he changed his mind and said, "You're becoming too serious."

"Me?" I felt a shameful confusion washing over me. "What have I done wrong?"

"Nothing," he answered. "You haven't done anything wrong."

"Then what is it?"

"I saw Scott over the break."

"Scott?"

"Miles Gloriosus."

It was a devastating admission once I realized what he had implied. Jealousy, anger, disappointment, loss, tumbled through my consciousness. I felt myself washed away from the safe place I had inhabited with Cliff. I didn't know how to think because there were too many thoughts crashing through my mind, and within them was not an ounce of acceptance, compassion, or forgiveness. I felt wronged and humiliated.

"We can still be friends," he added.

"Friends?"

"I still want to see you," he said, trying to soften the blow. "I still want to hang out with you now and then."

"Now and then?"

"Lots of guys sleep around with other guys," Cliff said. "You can see other guys, too."

I sat there wanting to cry, but I kept my composure, reaching for the sandwich that was on my tray. I took a bite, but my throat was dry. I chewed and coughed to deflect my feelings, chugging down my misery with a sip of soda. I was astonished by the hurt I felt—how far I had traveled in such a short space of time.

"Do you hate me?" Cliff asked after a while. He had not eaten anything on his plate since I had arrived at the table.

"No," I answered. "I'm not that kind of guy."

I mentioned earlier that my coming out was not my reason for writing this story, though it—and Cliff—were important elements in the shape of it. That afternoon in the cafeteria was not the end of Cliff. In fact, we went back to my room where we had sex—soft, tender, passionate make-up sex—more intense than our first times together—and afterwards he cried in my arms. He apologized for "hurting me," though the distance of time lets me now see that he was also hurting himself. I always felt that he loved me in the way that I loved him and his fear of it got the better of him. But at the time I didn't know what to do to make him want to stay with me, what else I had to give him, or even where I was headed myself. A problem I realize I still have today.

I found it harder to process a "best friend" who did not want to be a "best friend" and it left me wounded, but in the days, hours, and minutes without Cliff I felt exposed and alone. I was not a hunter of anything or anyone—success, money, friends, sex. I was not the sort of guy to steal or lie my way into some extra cash nor was I the sort to cruise to find a sexual hookup with anyone—and I had no desire for money earned dishonestly and even less for anonymous relationships, and, in truth, at the time the latter concept baffled me more than the first. My sexual attraction to a man included the desire to know something more of him: his name, his background, and his personal history. I wanted to understand his drama before I became a part of it.

But I did feel the need to understand my feelings better and move beyond Cliff, and to understand what being "gay" meant or could mean to me, so when I was finished with my finals and papers and Cliff had left for the Christmas holiday break to return to be with his family, I tried to make a few visits alone to the clubs I had been introduced to, but I couldn't ever seem to progress from parking the car and walking to the club entrance, which was how I found myself outside the bleak concrete building that housed Lady Belle's Legacy one cold evening. I knew that David emceed a weekly drag show on the weekends, but I wasn't interested in the show—I only wanted to talk to David. I was ready to cry on his shoulder and have him draw me to his chest and pat me on the head and tell me everything would be okay, just as I had witnessed him do many times with others. In the parking lot I found the lime green Volkswagen Beetle that David drove around town and left a short note beneath his front windshield wiper. On a folded piece of paper I wrote "Hi, remember me? I would love to get together and talk!" along with my name and phone number, then worried as I drove away if the wind would blow the note away or the mist that seemed to hover over all of Atlanta that evening would wash away my plea.

David didn't call me the next day or the next and I moved through a space of feeling confused and alienated, the loneliness haunting me until one evening after I finished my shift at the grocery store, I drove again to Lady Belle's Legacy and sat in my car for what felt like hours, watching the entrance, trying to judge my intentions as worthwhile or worthless. I finally made my way inside, hiding in a pocket of darkness until the laughter and music pulled me slowly to the far counter of the bar. I ordered a beer and watched the parade of drag queens coming and going off stage, confused by the flurry of lines spit at a microphone, but at times forgetting my mission of seeking out the unlikely friendship of David. I stayed until the lights flickered for "last call," and was lingering again in a darkened corner hoping no one was paying attention that I was around, waiting to spot David leaving the club so I could casually walk up to him and say hello and hope that he would remember the note I had left him and detect my broken-winged expression and take me to heart. The club emptied out and the lights were brightened as a man started sweeping the floor and tipping the chairs to the tops of the tables. A short woman with big red hair and a long, leathery face—Lady Belle, herself, I would later learn—approached me and said in a gruff tone, "We're closing up now, Sugah. Time to leave."

I responded, anxiously, with, "I was looking for David. I wanted to say 'hi.'"

"David?" she responded. "You mean, LaVilla?"

She caught my nod without even giving me a second look and asked the man who was sweeping, "LaVilla still in the joint? There's a boy looking for her."

I was embarrassed to be referred to as a "boy," but the man stopped sweeping and said that he thought LaVilla had slipped out long ago. I was astonished that I had not seen David leaving the club because I had been studying every face that had passed by me. I felt a shadow growing larger behind me and heard a deep, raspy voice ask, "What you want with that tired old queen?"

Approaching me was a big man with wide shoulders and a barrel chest, older, probably in his mid-thirties, dressed in a sweatshirt and jeans and which made him look like giant teddy bear. He was putting on a baseball cap to cover his shortly cut dark hair. He had an open, round face, a thin nose, big ears, and large expressive brown eyes. I saw too quickly that he was wearing pink fingernail polish and he saw right back my confusion and nervousness because of it.

"I just wanted to say 'hi,' that's all," and I turned to leave the club.

"Wait a second, Honey Child," he answered and with two giant steps was right beside me. "Nobody's gonna hurt you. You're not a runaway, are ya?"

"Runaway?"

"From home? You need a place to stay?"

"No," I shook my head. "That's not it."

Now he was in front of me, gently blocking my way out of the club. "Okay, well, that's a start, Babycakes."

"I just wanted to say 'hi,' that's all," I repeated.

"Well, I'll tell her—him—David—when I see... him." He was leaning down, trying to catch my eyes and when he did, he kept them there, saying, "Look, we all meet up at a joint down the street for a bite after the show. LaVilla might just be there too tonight. Want to join us?"

I asked him where the place was and realized I had been there several times before not knowing it was a place where... well, I could find other guys like myself, though I knew it all the time but had been unwilling to recognize it and successfully seize the opportunity of meeting someone.

I followed the large man outside and in the dark of the parking lot he offered to drive me to the diner, but when I mentioned that I would meet him there because I had my own car, he said, "You're not gonna chicken out on me, are ya, Honey Bee?"

It was odd hearing the familiar endearments usually uttered by my mother and other elderly Southern ladies used by this large, handsome man, but it endowed him with an easy charm and an accessibility his size might have otherwise thwarted. When I didn't give him an answer quick enough, he said, "I don't know your name, do I?"

I introduced myself and he said his name was Peaches.

"Peaches?" I asked in a high, surprised voice as I shook his hand.

"Well, it's really Sincerely Peaches, but everyone just calls me Peaches."

As I headed toward my car, I heard him yell out to me: "Now don't disappoint me, Honey Child. I'll be waiting for you at the front door."

Steve Parker
aka
Sincerely Peaches

Peaches was waiting for me at the front door of Dunk 'n' Dine, a small diner not far from the club. As we made our way to a table, I looked around the small diner for David, but I didn't see him, but Peaches introduced me to a table of his friends—a group of boisterous gay men who had been out dancing—as we headed for a table near the back window.

"Now, don't be jealous, Miss Thang," Peaches laughed as he accepted a menu from an elderly waiter with spikey white hair who stood in front of our table with pursed lips and a hand on a hip. "My new friend here is not fresh meat."

"Well, *you* certainly aren't," the waiter said to Peaches.

"Honey Child, meet Miss Bobby Ray, the oldest queen in town."

I smiled and nodded, but before I could say anything, Bobby Ray was telling me, "Be careful about this old broad. Once she knows one little thing about you, she thinks she owns you."

"Ignore this crazy fool who doesn't know how to wear an apron," Peaches said. "You don't mind if we have a bit to eat, do you? I worked up such a sweat on stage tonight. I'm famished." He turned to Bobby Ray and ordered the "usual," which turned out to be a stack of pancakes. But there was more ado because Peaches wanted blueberry syrup, not raspberry or strawberry or any other berry syrup but the blueberry kind. And then followed a request for a side order of sausages, beef not pork.

"One dick or two?" Bobby Ray asked.

"You know what they say," Peaches smiled. "Two dicks are better than one."

"I'll tell the chef not to overcook them tonight, though it might not be possible in your case."

I was more nervous than hungry but ordered a grilled cheese sandwich which Peaches insisted I add bacon to.

"A growing boy like you needs all the meat you can stuff inside you," he said, giving me a wink.

Bobby Ray gave Peaches a hard look and said, "When did you start playing the top?"

"You're such a doll, Bobby Ray. Now be gone before a house falls on you."

My eyes followed Bobby Ray as he made his way to the front register and gave the order to a cook behind a tall counter. I looked around again for David but still didn't see him.

"Lots of evil queens here," Peaches said. "But not the one you're looking for. Now tell me, Honey Child. How do you know LaVilla Débris?"

And so I unraveled the sad tale of my heartbreak from Cliff, glad for a sympathetic ear even as Bobby Ray and our arriving food provided flippant distractions. At the story's conclusion, Peaches said, "First love is always the hardest to get over. You just need to find a way to knock him out of your head. Both heads."

I didn't fully understand the reference to two heads because I thought he was referring to Cliff as well; the slang was going way over my head, so I stayed quiet.

"Did you see the show tonight?" Peaches asked.

I nodded and he kept talking, "So you saw my number? I was the one in the sensible outfit—with the white gloves and the pillbox hat."

"That was you?" I answered. "You looked…

"Taller? Prettier?"

"Smaller," I answered.

He let out a large laugh, the same kind of laugh he had delivered on stage. "Contouring," he said. "I can give you as many pointers as you need."

We talked through the meals—or Peaches did most of the talking. "Come along, young man," Peaches said, when we finished and he had paid the bill. "I am going to provide you with an education."

Peaches, aka Steve Parker, lived in the basement of a building on Ponce de Leon near Highland, in an apartment fashioned around concrete walls painted "peach blossom pink." It was an extraordinary space without rooms, cold and damp, a labyrinth of wigs, mannequins, antique mirrors, and moveable racks of costumes and gowns which led to a king-sized water bed with a tall wicker headboard threaded with peacock feathers. My education began that night, or, rather, that morning, as I bobbed and steadied myself on the springy water-filled mattress as Peaches instructed me to hold back my orgasm as he worked me over with his mouth and hands.

Peaches refused to allow me to attach sentimentality to sex. "No puppy dog eyes," he said after our first and second times together, and then as my sexual education progressed and our friendship became closer, added, "We are not boyfriends. We are boy friends. There is a big difference to that."

All this went on behind David's back. He had never called me and as far as I knew no one had mentioned to him that I had looked for him at the club, though a few nights later while I was waiting by the bar for Peaches to go to the diner, David saw me and asked me where Cliff was. My flustered reaction must have given everything away—that I was still in love with Cliff and that I was catting around without him. I made up a lie that Cliff was studying—knowing it probably wasn't a lie, but I didn't know *what* Cliff was doing because

Cliff didn't want me to know. When Peaches arrived a moment later, she comically brushed David aside, greeted me as "Darling!" and kissed me on both cheeks.

David was no sucker for such theatrics. The gestures were enough for him to know what was going on between me and Peaches. He rolled his giant eyes up toward his taller friend and said, "Peaches, Dearest One, don't be a fool."

Peaches responded, "LaVilla, Darling Dearest, only a fool would hesitate."

A week or so later, Peaches suddenly announced my education could go no further and he led me into the bathhouse in the strip shopping center across from Lady Belle's club, abandoning me before I had completely discarded my clothes.

And I confess that I was soon better at being an inquisitive gay man than at being a serious college student. I discovered that the challenges of my classes were no match for the distractions of learning more about the nuances of gay life, or, rather, learning more about my attraction toward men. Everything that touched my hands and moved across my vision now seemed sexually charged and potentially homosexual. For a while I coasted by on reading study guides in the campus bookstore or excerpting the bound honors theses I discovered in an aisle of the top floor of the main campus library, but soon I was missing classes to catch up on sleep or working extra hours at the grocery store in order to be able to afford to wander the hallway of the newly discovered bathhouse.

The baths were a maze of dark hallways and strange smells (sometimes ammonia, other times mildew or something that had not been cleaned for a long while). Peaches always said it was best to frequent such establishments "a little bit loopy, so you're thinking more about a stranger's hose than what's squishing between your toes." One corridor opened up into a large, dark room of bunks and stools and chairs, and then another corridor led to a series of doors that opened to dimly lit private rooms where men waited lying on their stomachs or backs, depending on the role they wanted to perform that night. It was never the crowded and thematic spectacle I would witness in later years in New York and LA, but there was usually enough action to prevent me from leaving and there was always some guy who could boost my lonely ego by slipping me a business card on my way out and asking me for another time together.

And it was an ongoing education, learning how one man gave a blow job, how another fingered an ass, how another would clutch and stroke his dick. But I confess that most of the times I spent in the arms of a stranger I was often thinking of Cliff. And when I wasn't thinking of him, I was wondering what Peaches was up to.

And then one icy morning in February, Cliff and I ran into David as we were walking across campus together to the cafeteria. David stopped us and caught us up on gossip we didn't know already. Although David had graduated from the university two years before, he still had deep roots on campus and he told us that Neal, the balding graduate student, had left his wife of two years because of his affair with Melissa, the girl who had played Dolly Levi. David avoided reprimanding me of my trysts with Peaches, possibly because he believed the gossip had not made its way to Cliff, but he had also heard of my ongoing romps with Doug, a dental student I had met at the Locker Room. ("Yes, Honey Bunch, Mama knows all," he said, and then sang a snatch of the Disneyland kid's tune: "It's a small, small world....") We had an awkward laugh because Cliff had also had a thing with Doug, then David mentioned that Austin was now playing piano in the bar of a snooty downtown hotel and we would have to make a date soon "to crash that lousy gin joint." As we were parting, David suddenly turned and asked Cliff if he wanted to be part of a new act he was planning for Lady Belle's Legacy. "It's a dog-eat-dog biz," David said and comically rolled his eyes. "I gotta keep up with them other bitches." David explained that Coco, a leggy, muscular, caramel-skinned drag queen, was now beginning her routine in a gorilla suit, then unzipping it to step out and sing and dance with a pair of loin-clad muscular warriors, "like she's Sheena, Queen of the Jungle or someone extra special."

Cliff said that David's idea sounded like it had "potential" and that they would work out a rehearsal time by phone later that week, though I knew as we walked away he was not too keen on the idea of dancing at The Legacy. Still, he did show up one night to rehearse with David and another fellow named Brian whom I had often noticed dancing at Backstreet. David had decided he wanted to perform his new number, "Steam Heat," a flashy song from the Broadway musical *The Pajama Game*, flanked by two guys dancing in a slow, jazzy style. When Brian bowed out after that first rehearsal ("Hey, man, this just isn't me," he told David), Cliff convinced David that since the routine he had in mind was a slow and simple soft shoe, I might be the perfect choice to be the second guy, and one night on the phone I was told that they wanted to try me out, as if I were a costume they were not quite certain would fit or might not like to wear for anyone else to see even after it had been appropriately tailored.

"Darling, it's not really dancing," David cooed to me on the phone. "More like acting like you're dancing."

"And you don't want me to sing?"

"Of course not, Honey Bunch. Just smile and be your gorgeous dazzling self."

We rehearsed for two days in a small room upstairs at the student center. David was a hurricane of pop cultural references—MGM musical costumes, Bob Fosse dance steps, Busby Berkeley special effects. Each new movement I learned was full of historical importance—"Move your hand just so," he said, "and everyone will think of Liza."

Though the routine was easy enough, there were other obstacles to my performing at The Legacy. My costume was a black derby, white gloves, a black bowtie, and a black sequined vest with a matching thong, and in retrospect, blood rushes to my cheeks in embarrassment to admit this, and that I actually performed (and enjoyed performing) this pseudo-go-go boy routine. Cliff and I were used simply as objects of enticement. (David even padded our thongs to make us look *more* well-endowed.) I am proud to admit, however, even at this humble, old, and out-of-shape age, that I was thin enough in those days to carry off this farce, since whatever muscle tone my physique might have lacked at that point in my life was made up for by the sheer brashness of my youth.

I didn't see Peaches again until the night we performed the routine at Lady Belle's Legacy, as Cliff and I were backstage dressing, or, rather, mostly undressing.

"Sugah, you don't need no rouge," Peaches said to me. "Your cheeks are rosy enough."

"No touching the merchandise," David batted Peaches away.

LaVilla Débris

"Honey, I already done had a sample of that," Peaches answered. "You know, I'm always one leg ahead of you."

The number was a big hit the night we performed it at Lady Belle's Legacy and we were asked to repeat it the following weekend. By the time the next weekend arrived, however, Cliff was adamant about *not* performing it again. The evening of our first performance at The Legacy, Cliff had met and gone home with a lawyer from Decatur who had turned into something of a stalker after he discovered Cliff didn't want to see him again. David tried his best "Big Mama" and "Sweetheart" and "Honey Bunch" routines to convince Cliff otherwise, but to no avail. He didn't want to attract "any more psychos."

But the show did go on. Instead of replacing Cliff in the number, David moved me slightly to the background and hit me with a pink spotlight; I danced alone while he sang his number, dressed in his, or rather *her*, frilly and prim Victorian garb that she slowly stripped away in a dramatic-comic fashion. This, too, was a big hit at Lady Belle's Legacy and it was how I found my way into the weekend lineup of performers, three performances on Friday and Saturdays and two on Sundays. As I recall now, I was not paid for any of my appearances, not even "a little extra something" from the tip bucket that the "Spectacular Sisters" passed around the audience after the show. All I got was an occasional free post-show drink courtesy of a hunky bartender that I had one night in the parking lot behind the building, my first "public encounter," and the truth of the matter, and this is the honest, raw-boned truth of my life, the applause and attention awere all the remuneration I required.

I did not rate a changing room at The Legacy, either, nor even a chair or a stool in front of the long, mirrored wall that served as the dressing room the "Sisters" shared

Holly DeVine

backstage. Many of the guys arrived fully transformed into their queenly personas before they performed at the club, preferring the better lighting of their home vanity mirrors over the dim backstage light, cracked reflections, and splintered wood shelving. David would usually show up with his makeup done and his hair already plastered beneath a skullcap. He zoomed cross town in his green Beetle wearing a baseball cap, using the small backstage corridor to tighten his corset, step into his gown, and strap on his high heels, before putting the finishing touches on his eyes and lips and positioning his blonde wig in place so as to become his alter ego. I usually gravitated to where David was sitting to shed my jeans and T-shirt beside him, as if he could offer me protection from the other drag queens, but my disrobing was usually met with a theatrical "ahhhhh" or "ooooh" from one or all of the ladies, and more often than not, David, now regally transformed into fabulously trashy LaVilla Débris, would bring attention to my undressing routine by pretending to slap my exposed ass cheek or flattening the sequins of my jockstrap into place, and saying to the others present backstage, "Look at me, Sweethearts, I've got the best seat in the house!"

Luckily, there was a "no touching" policy backstage among the performers, so what could have been an awkward scenario was always a highly comic one instead, with a chorus line of half-men/half-women air kissing and fake slapping each other. Someone was always elbowing for more room, electric shavers and hair-dryers drowning out comments so that they had to be screamed a second time, and someone was always shooting hairspray or blowing cigarette smoke in a direction it didn't belong, only to pucker her lips and apologize and then do it again.

Sincerely Peaches

For the most part the drag queens backstage were a bitter, complaining crowd, though I write this with more affection than judgment, because the objections and protests to the small quarters were lodged with an amicable campiness. They were "Sisters," after all. And there were some deep-seated friendships at work backstage—David and Peaches—no one called him Steve—had once been boyfriends, or as David explained while Peaches elbowed his way through the space one evening, "Queen Dong over there is the one who first pawed me." Peaches was more tight-lipped about our own tryst. "Your secrets are safe with me," she told me that first weekend I was at the club with Cliff, "until there is no reason for them not to remain secret."

Charlie Winters, aka Chanelle Tempest, who did a routine as Carole King and Janis Joplin, and Paul Ramsey, aka Sabrina Flair, who imitated Judy, Liza, and sometimes Barbra, had gone to elementary school together in Florida. Coco shared an apartment with a bartender who worked at the club on weeknights. But there were also some hard and cold animosities at work amongst these would-be divas— one night Sabrina had introduced her dermatologist, a short, stocky, exotic-looking man named Yaman Najarian and nicknamed "Doc," to Holly DeVine. Holly, formerly known as Michael B. Terrill, was so small and fragile and flakey-acting that she seemed to channel the ghost of Marilyn Monroe, had turned her need for medical advice into a volatile affair of cash and drugs with Doc, which left Sabrina curt and resentful.

But the deepest rift backstage was between those who performed and those who lipped. I could make no distinction for the better or worse between the two distinct forms of performing at the club—Peaches' flawless lip-synching to a Petula Clark or Dusty Springfield song was

Sabrina Flair

just as entertaining to me as watching Holly sing "When Love Goes Wrong" in her own fragile, whispery voice. Both sides of this ongoing war thought the other side phony and talentless, each side calling the other as far from the real thing as a girl could be.

I found the chasm that occurred offstage more strange and interesting—the way lives were lived outside the club, out in the parking lot after the performances and in the daylight at the shopping malls and grocery stores and apartment buildings in the city. There was an intense resentment against the ladies who lived and passed themselves off as "real women" among those who only dressed up for a paying audience and had no desire to alter their god-given male gift. There was never any question that David was a guy who dressed up as a woman for the stage, and the same went for Peaches—who liked to stand onstage and tell his "fruit-pickers" all about his fake boobs—sometimes they were water balloons, which he would threaten to toss into the audience, but mostly they were edible fruit—oranges or apples or peaches, and if he had the crowd shaking with laughter, he might reach into his bra, lift one out and take a bite. I once noticed him outside the club dressed in jeans and a flannel shirt, pumping gas at the self-service island on Clifton Road, but I didn't realize it was him till he waved his peach-colored nails at me and arched an eyebrow and said in his campiest voice, "Creampuff, Honey Child, what butch fellow drug you out so far from home?" Coco, too, lived as a guy, or as I heard, lived with two roommates who were both gay men, and held down three jobs including one as a part-time janitor of an office building on Clairmont. He was rumored to be "over-endowed" and "swung both ways." I remember one night when a true girl wandered backstage at the club, a hippy-looking frizzy-haired chick wearing a flowered peasant blouse, who flirted shamelessly with Coco (sticking her tongue in his mouth and slipping her hand into the crotch of his leotard). The other Sisters in the room turned sour and defensive over the intrusion and the breach of the "no-touching policy." Coco enjoyed creating problems backstage—in fact, she thrived on upstaging the other performers there as much as in front of the spotlights. According to David, Coco was the highest-paid and busiest of the Legacy broads *off* the stage—there was always some guy (or even a group of guys) wanting to hook up with Coco, and, well, party through the night, and Coco was paid well because she knew how to party (and party well).

Sabrina also had her little entourage of admirers backstage, mostly the older or lonelier men in the audience, who wanted to meet her and tell her how precisely and accurately and uncannily she reminded them of Judy because they had seen Judy perform at Carnegie Hall or the Palace or the Palladium or the Talk of the Town. (Sabrina's best number was the one where she sat on a stool beneath a single bright-white spotlight, dressed in a white shirt and black leotard and tearfully lipped "The Man That Got Away.") David told me one night when we went out after the show for pancakes at the IHOP that Sabrina was one confused little girl. Or boy. "One minute she wants to do implants, injections, and have an operation," he said, "and the next she knows she can't live without her biggest asset. If you ask me, that chick is A Train Wreck Waiting to Happen."

Sabrina's confusions, however, did not hold a candle to those of Holly DeVine. Holly was twenty-six, five-feet-six, and had just enough extra flesh to keep her body looking soft and feminine. Holly had grown her real hair out long and bleached it blonde; she kept her fingernails long, painted, and manicured at all times, and wherever she walked she was followed by a heavy cloud of perfume. She still used the padded bra she discovered six years before in the lingerie department of Woolworth's in Little Rock, and she learned to hide her "candy" with fabric and a strong roll of duct tape. She went out of the club dressed as a woman, shopped in grocery stores wearing big movie-star sunglasses and expensive scarves over her hair to protect her teased and sprayed curls. In many respects Holly was fearless in this regard—to go out like this at that time and in that region of the country was a big gamble, but Holly's biggest asset was that she believed she already was a woman—and she was tiny and delicate and pretty enough for most strangers to believe she was one, too. Holly wasn't completely satisfied with herself, however; she wanted hormones and implants and the operation that would permanently alter her gender "just like Christine did," she would whisper (meaning, of course, Christine Jorgensen, the famous man who became a more famous woman), and Holly had turned to Dr. Najarian to achieve her hopes. Dr. Najarian was not skilled in that regard, or at least that was what Sabrina said, but the good doctor pumped up Holly's dreams and kept them fluid through a host of injections and drugs that he had access to.

Najarian was also deeply attracted to Holly—it was clear to everyone at The Legacy how protective and jealous and needy he was of her. He seldom left her alone, unless he needed to go to meet somebody to "pick something special up." There were all sorts of rumors about Doc. That he was not a doctor, that he was working for the Mafia, that he was selling drugs from Mexico. Peaches flat out didn't like him. "He's not one of us," she said. "Even if he talks dick."

They were always fighting backstage—Holly usually wanted Doc to get her something and he was resistant because he knew she wanted some time alone and away from him, and then if she got someone else to get her whatever it was she wanted—sometimes me, like a soda or a bobby pin or tissues—Doc would grow furious and batter Holly with insults, saying she was flirting and leading me (or another guy) on, and she had promised, gotten down on her knees and sworn to him, that she would never, ever, do that kind of thing again. Holly would scream and tell Doc that she hated him. It was the kind of hatred that comes with intense desire. I once witnessed him slapping her with the back of his hand while they were getting into his car in the parking lot, and there were times when Sabrina or Coco would leave the dressing room because they did not want to be caught up in their fury. Peaches and David often broke up their spats, telling Najarian to wait in the hallway because the dressing room was for performers only, "not the low-life scum hanger-on backstage Johnnies like you," as Peaches would yell (and, since she towered over him, Doc would reluctantly leave, though not moving as far away as the rest of us would have preferred).

"You better watch your back, girlfriend," Najarian would threaten Peaches, from the doorway.

"I'm not your girlfriend, Mister," Peaches would snarl back. "Never was, never will be. Ever in your lifetime! You don't deserve something this *good*."

"Excuse me for mistaking a piece of trash for something with class," Doc would lob back. And on and on it would go, before someone took one of them to another room.

I was not at the club to witness the harshest exchange between Najarian and Holly, which occurred one night about a month after David had revealed his new "Steam Heat" number. Najarian thought it was time that Holly get some new energy and numbers in her act like the rest of the drag queens were doing and Holly had been teary most of the night, according to the way I heard it from Peaches the following weekend. The fighting had continued through the show and out into the parking lot afterward, with Holly becoming more and more defensive about her "real art," trying to explain to Doc how difficult it was to perform live to a recorded track blaring out through a sound speaker she was not even standing next to and make it all seem believable and entertaining. In anger, Holly swatted at Najarian and missed, but Doc pushed Holly into the row of trash cans that lined the back of the building. Holly twisted her ankle in the fall and screechingly complained as she lifted herself up off the ground that she would call the police and file a restraining order against him. She then took the lid of the tin trash can and swung it at Najarian and hit him in the eye. Najarian, startled and enraged, pushed Holly back against the wall and somehow broke two of her ribs and her left wrist, though I heard later, through David, that he had also tried to strangle her and she had stopped him with a desperate kick in the groin.

Najarian's cut was deep and bloody and soon they were both cooing, "Oh, baby," and "Oh, no, sweetie," to each other and Najarian was driving both of them to the emergency room. David had even augmented the story by saying that when he spoke to Holly on the phone, she had told him that Najarian was not even a real doctor. "He's a phony-baloney," Holly had whispered to David as though she were Garbo playing out the last moments of *Camille*. Najarian couldn't use any professional clout to get them seen quickly at the emergency room because he had none. He left Holly alone when he overheard a receptionist calling the police to question them. Holly fled as well, and used a pay phone to call her cousin in Roswell to pick her up, and it wasn't until the following morning that she was finally checked into a private clinic upstate. "I thought I was gonna die," Holly said when she called David three days later. "He wanted me to die. He wanted to kill me. I've never had anyone want to kill me. I don't understand. Why would he want to kill me?"

David enjoyed being a sympathetic fairy godmother, a "Long Island Babushka" in residence to "save all the silly Daisy Maes from self-destruction." He would spend hours giving his new charges fashion and beauty tips, even though his act was more a comedy routine than the imitation of a glamorous diva. He knew the best glue to keep false eyelashes in place, how to conceal a natural eyebrow without having to shave it off, how to best tuck the "candy" away and tape a chest to form cleavage. "Somebody's got to teach these little bitches how to be feminine," he once told me. "The first time I did drag—not that long ago, mind you, moi's sophomore year in college—I thought I looked fab-u-lous. But Mary, I was really a booger mess. I thank the Good Lady Above that Miss Sincerely Peaches gave me a stern talking to, otherwise I would still be thinking I was LaVilla Divine."

Miss Sincerely Peaches was an expert on hair, having learned his trade as a barber during a two-year stint in the Navy. "Honey Child, I was the lucky girl who got to massage all those luscious scalps before I ran a razor over them." The Navy had been Peaches' way of "getting out of Tullahoma, Tennessee and seeing the world," though he never got any farther than Charleston and "a few miles beneath Miss Bermuda's Triangle." While on leave in Atlanta, he danced with another boy at the Joy Lounge on Ponce de Leon and decided he was having too much fun to stay in the military. He found work as a hairdresser in "a cheap dive near the

Pershing Point Hotel," and was inspired to do drag himself after setting the wigs for "all the big queens who found their way to me." Peaches was a walking history book of camp life and gay Atlanta. He recommended the second-floor men's room at the Sears in Buckhead, just beyond the small appliances, "if you want a superhot quickie," and thought the Farmer's Market was the only place in town "to find a decent, honest man who would stay over for the night." He knew the best Bette Davis lines from *All About Eve*; *Dark Victory*; *Jezebel*; *Now, Voyager*; and *What Ever Happened to Baby Jane?* Peaches had met Liberace and Paul Lynde when he had performed at Hollywood Hots, the drag club across the street from The Legacy, and he had had the privilege of having his photo taken backstage with Liza Minnelli at the Civic Center, when she brought her tour to town.

Sabrina had met both Liza *and* Lorna Luft, and for an entire summer she had performed as Judy Garland with a cast of puppets at Six Flags Over Georgia, an amusement park on the west side of the city. Paul's mother, up from Florida for a visit, had thought it was her son's proudest moment and the most thrilling show she had ever seen. She had known Sabrina was "that way" since he was eight and he had staged a one-person production of *The Wizard of Oz* on roller skates in the family's carport. Sabrina was the Sister who saved the day backstage when a gown needed mending or a feather boa snapped apart. She always had a sewing kit and safety pins, promising to work "a little magic" before stepping on stage, using the skills her mamma had taught her.

Even Holly could be a good teacher when she wasn't married to the mirror or stuck in Doc's orbit. "You can never be too thin, too rich, or too careful," she once told me, which, I thought when I first heard it, made her sound very sophisticated. Holly's favorite color was blue, but she chose the color of her outfits to "psychologically depict the mood of the song. Red is a sexy, aggressive color," she explained to me. "Nobody forgets you in a red dress." And Holly was seldom forgotten. She had never been farther than New Orleans, where a hotel clerk had beaten her up just because he felt like it. She had beaten up another drag queen in Tallahassee and had been arrested in Birmingham "for looking like I was doing something when I wasn't doing a thing." Peaches always said trouble was out looking for Holly, but she said that about Sabrina, Coco, and Chanelle Tempest, too, but I think we all believed it most about Holly.

I've always considered my past life in Atlanta as an educational time, though there were plenty of things going on at The Legacy that I was not aware of at the time—narc agents in the parking lot, hustlers at the bar, coke lines being snorted in the bathroom. It wasn't that I was looking at any of this life through rose-tinted glasses, but in many respects I've always believed my naïveté is what saved me. I never developed my own drag queen alter ego, though it was often the subject of many conversations I had with those who already had one. I admired all of my new "sisters" for their courage and pride, wishing I could channel even just a shadow of their brashness and stand up for myself, but I always felt a bit more like an outsider watching the show and never really a part of the drama—or fun. Once Peaches met me for brunch at a pizza place near campus and showed up in her bright pink Chanel knockoff and white gloves. "It takes a lot of work to look this cheap," she said to both me and the waiter when she sat down at the booth, then she turned to a table of gawking sorority girls and said, "Girls, need any help with *the boys*?"

I had never seen Miss Sincerely Peaches done up in drag outside The Legacy and in the full light of day—and I have to admit he—or she—was an astonishing creation. The detail behind her eye shadow alone must have taken him hours to perfect. When Peaches had asked me to meet him the night before, he had told me he had to be in my neighborhood for a birthday party for a "gentleman friend." I didn't know that meant she was *to be* the party. (Silly me.)

That afternoon, as our conversation rambled between Lady Belle Lemmonds' new policy of "no free booze for the Sisters" because profits were scarce, and David's new fixation on getting Najarian banned from the club, Peaches folded her hands together, batted her eyelashes, and asked, "Baby Boy, why don't you have a serious beau?"

"I'm not talking about that boy you like to dance with, Honey Bunch," Peaches added. "I'm talking about a real serious beau who can't live without you. Someone who adores you the way I do."

"I guess I'm still waiting to meet him," I answered, then, feeling as if I ought to say something about Cliff, to defend him—or defend my interest in him, said "We're good friends."

"That boy's not your friend," Peaches said with an annoyance that surprised me. "He's just lonely and using you to keep from being alone. A true friend will walk through fire for you and I know that boy wouldn't do it. Trust your Sister on this one, Mary. When did he ever call you up and ask you how you felt or offer to do you a favor? LaVilla and I have our differences, but do you know she saw this hat in a thrift shop and just plunked down the money for it and gave it to me without even thinking twice or asking me for a penny for it? Because she knew—he just *knew* it was me. That boy wouldn't even buy you a pack of cigarettes.

Paul Ramsey
aka
Sabrina Flair

Those girls at the club bring each other eyeliner and rouge and hairspray. I let David borrow my panty hose all the time, even though he stretches it all out of whack. I trust and love those girls and they love me back. And Honey, I style all of their wigs for *nothing*. That's true friendship for you. Would that little boy do that for you?"

I knew, as absurd as it sounded, there was a lot of truth behind what Peaches was saying and the truth hurt. I knew Cliff didn't love me in the way that I loved him. My eyes welled up with dismay. Peaches stretched out her hand across the table and said, "Baby Boy, you know something? You'd make a beautiful girl. Has anybody ever told you that? With your cheekbones, and high neck, and those gray eyes, you'd be drop-dead gorgeous in full drag. Come to think of it, though, maybe you shouldn't try it. You could end up like Holly DeVine. Now that's a mess. If you went out and got tits you'd have to learn to sleep with them, wouldn't you? And we wouldn't want that to ever happen, would we? We like you just the way you are—yummy, yummy, yummy!"

I didn't walk away from Cliff and give up our friendship; instead, I turned myself into the kind of friend that I wished he might have been for me. It was early spring when Cliff's mother called his dorm room to tell him that his father had died of a stroke. I held him in my arms as he cried and absorbed the shock, and watched him pack a small suitcase. When I said goodbye to him as I dropped him off at the airport, I did not expect that it was the end of us—our friendship or our pseudo-relationship. He was only going to be away for "a while"—an indeterminate while—but I always expected he was coming back.

But his absence left me adrift—with Cliff gone I felt more alone than I had when I transferred at the beginning of the school year, and I fought hard to balance myself by maintaining my class load and keeping up with my studies, and then unhinged myself even further with the serious notion of dropping out when I realized I had to make a work shift at the grocery store. When the auditions rolled around for another campus theatrical production, this time *Bye, Bye, Birdie*, I did not bother to show up. By then I had successfully woven myself deeply into the fabric of gay Atlanta nightlife.

So I turned to David to fill the void that Cliff's absence created. David had replaced his "Steam Heat" number at The Legacy with a new song that did not include a part for me, so I often sat backstage with him before he emceed the weekly amateur drag night, or met him for a late breakfast at a coffee shop in our neighborhood. David would detail the latest comings and goings of the performers and clientele of The Legacy with the same glee as Cliff had used when lifting the stereo needle to play a song he wanted me to hear. Coco was now involved with an older society woman who thought he should stop performing at the club, and Lady Belle, the namesake and manager who was seldom around when I was there, was showing up more and more to see Trashetta, a drag comic who had made a big splash on amateur night by not even singing a note (or, as Peaches later told me, not singing a note *right*). David was incredibly jealous of Trashetta, worried that Lady Belle might be grooming the comic to take over the emcee roles he had always done. Holly had not returned from her upstate exile with her cousin, and Chanelle Tempest had left her club in Mobile to fill Holly's spot. Dr. Najarian, though, had reappeared to court Sabrina backstage, and their rekindled affair was becoming as hostile as the one he had had with Holly, and now it was Chanelle who went around warning Sabrina to watch out or something awful was going to happen, not just to her, but to any and all of them.

Doc warmed to me one night at the club when I asked him where I could buy a joint or two. (My reliable supply had disappeared with Cliff.) Najarian told me he had several grades with varying prices and I asked him for one that was inexpensive but would do the job I wanted it to do. Our business was transacted a few minutes later backstage by the toilets, but out front in the main room of the club, during a break between performances, he sat beside me at the bar and we talked about the weather—we had just made it through an unusually windy week and everyone had a story to tell about freaky gusts and falling branches, snapping power lines, and accidents on the road. Najarian explained how he had seen an uprooted tree fall on top of a parked car. "Not the way I want to die," he said and laughed. "No honor there."

Najarian wasn't simply the brusque, rude character I have thus far painted him to be, but a man molded by a desire to flee the low-paying factory jobs of the industrial northeast where his family had settled after leaving India. He only wanted what everyone wanted: to cash in as much as he could out of the American dream. He also wanted "to sleep with whomever I want to sleep with," which meant—as for many of us—he had arrived in the gay underworld after fleeing an unsupportive family. I cannot verify his medical training, but he was not without his generous qualities; some nights he brought gifts backstage for all of us to enjoy—a cassette tape of one his favorite albums, the latest issues of *GQ*, *Newsweek*, and *After Dark*, or a box of warm Krispy Kreme donuts just out of the oven of the store on Highland Avenue (even though LaVilla complained of enormous sugar flakes lodging in her throat before she performed).

I had something of a crush on Najarian—he was sexy in a hyper-butch way, with a swarthy, square jawline peppered with black stubble, deep brown eyes, a receding hairline, and a physique as compact and muscled as a bulldog's. By now I was obsessed with sex and how it differed from man to man. That night, as we sat talking about the natural power of the wind, I wondered what his body looked like undressed, how the black hairs on his chest felt, how his balls and cock dangled between his legs—and how he used them, how he fucked and whether he was a kisser. I would rather not admit that Doc was my intended conquest for that night. But the thought was there, at the back—and front—of my mind as we sat together at the bar and waited for Sabrina.

Sabrina sent word out to Doc via Lady Belle that she wasn't feeling well and would get a ride home with Peaches. Normally, this would have provoked a fight—which was why Sabrina did it—she liked the flare-up of attention Doc gave her so they could coo and cuddle afterward. But Doc replied, "Suit her," and made no effort to go backstage and convince her otherwise, and the two of us sat and talked about a flea market that had settled into a space at a strip mall on Piedmont (where it was rumored that Doc hung out and sold drugs) or joined in conversations as others passed by us. (Coco was trying to see if anyone knew of an all-night liquor store—he wanted to show up later someplace "with something special" and Lady Belle wouldn't sell him anything from the bar of the club.) At various times, Doc put his arm around my shoulder or grasped my wrist to emphasize his points—or, as everyone wisely interpreted, to brazenly display that "this guy is mine for the night."

One by one the ladies came out and said their goodbyes before heading out to the parking lot and the cars. David blew me off that night because he had a "protégé-in-training," a tall, awkward boy named Harry who he thought might make a more vivacious and outgoing drag queen once his inner diva had been released and applied to the outside of his face. Sabrina lingered at the bar pouting and posing, hoping Doc would change his mind, but I could tell he was glad to be rid of her. Peaches towered over us and scowled at me—he knew exactly what I was up to and called me out on it. "Honey Bunch, don't go picking up any trash you find lying on the street to eat just because you're hungry," he whispered in my ear. "A Baby Boy could get sick, you know. Hurt. *Poisoned.* I wouldn't want you to regret it."

I gave him a weak smile, which meant that I knew exactly what I was doing and where I was headed, and he grasped Sabrina by the elbow and lead her out of the club. A few others went by and gave us hugs and kisses or little squeezes of the arm and said good-night, then Najarian turned to me and said, "Come on, I got some good stuff you can try. Make you feel like you're Superman."

I left my car at the club and rode with Doc back to his apartment. He lived a few blocks away near the park in an apartment building that looked like it might have once been a motel, but inside his place, there was a sequence of dusty, cluttered rooms with a strange, stuffy smell, as if the dark yellow oil-based paint that had been used decades before on the walls had been heated up and was sweating. There was a minimal amount of furniture—folding chairs and card tables—and unopened boxes of what appeared to be medical supplies or electronic items such as radios and

Yaman Najarian
aka
Doc

stereos stacked in corners. The bed was a mattress on the floor, with more boxes serving as end tables, one of which held an alarm clock and a large bottle of skin lotion. The liquor was on a window shelf near the kitchen and the floor below it. Looking around me, I wondered how both Holly and Sabrina had viewed and accepted this—both had struck me as high-maintenance gals who would not put up with such sloppy surroundings. Doc pulled down a small tin box hidden behind a larger box, opened it, and handed me a joint. "Private stash," he said. "It'll make you fly."

He had his own eclectic collection of record albums—soundtracks from Marilyn Monroe, Audrey Hepburn, and Lena Horne movies alongside others with exotically dressed Indian women in provocative poses and holding Asian musical instruments on the jackets, and shelves full of reel-to-reels, eight-track tapes, and smaller cassettes, and after opening and closing several cases, he inserted a tape into his stereo system and Frank Sinatra began singing softly in his young and jazzy style.

Doc sat on the couch beside where I was sitting, reached over and took the joint from me and lit it, took a long toke, and then passed it back to me, fumbling with an ashtray on the coffee table while I took my first hit. He smiled and locked his eyes to mine and sang a lyric phrase along with Sinatra, then held his smile until he was ready for another hit. His teeth were small and white against his dark skin. His eyebrows were long, black, and bushy, except for a short point at the bridge of his nose and I wondered if he plucked the hairs that grew there, like all the drag queens at The Legacy did. "You don't seem like the kind of kid who should be hanging around that club," he said to me when Frank finished his song.

"What kind of kid is that?"

My guess was that Najarian was close to forty, which would make him twice my age. I mistook his age and foreign looks as making him suave and debonair. "Too young for the Sisters."

"The Sisters, or the brothers who like to dress up in their clothes?" I asked.

"I bet you would break *all* of their hearts," he said. "So you shouldn't try."

I didn't take it as a warning. Instead, I asked, "What should I try, then?"

I had hardly had a chance to be coy and flirtatious, nor had we finished our joint, when he leaned into me and clutched the back of my neck and pulled me into a kiss. And I didn't let him break away. I used both hands to hold his lips in place as he tugged at my sweater and jeans, and his hands found my skin. He clutched my hip and shifted my body so that his other hand could fondle my cock. I felt his smile when I unbuttoned his shirt and ran my fingers across the hair on his chest. We were both half undressed when he said, "I want you to break my heart. *Tonight.*"

He caught my face with both hands and whispered his instructions in my ear, before enclosing it with his lips and fluttering his tongue and making me squirm with pleasure. He wanted me to try to fuck him. I followed him into his bedroom, where we kicked off the rest of our clothes and wrestled onto the mattress. He wanted to be fucked, yes, but he also wanted to act out his unwillingness to be penetrated, using all of his strength and charm instead to attempt to fuck me. I had thought that he would want me to bottom for him as most guys I went home with did, though it occurred to me sometime during our tussle that he must have wanted me for the change in his usual scenario with Sabrina, where, I assumed, he was always the dominant top.

He was stronger than I was and wanted to prove it by pinning me by my wrists to the mattress and sitting on my chest. It was a ruse, of course, to make me startle him by leaning up and kissing the cleft of his neck, catching him off guard and wrestling him into submission. When he was on his back, his dick lay flat against his stomach—not jutting skyward like some guys I had been with—and I took it in my mouth at the same time as I lifted his legs over my shoulders. He arched his back away from the mattress and lifted his buttocks, and I cupped and kneaded him while he pleasantly "resisted" until he was ready to accept me.

The small, dark room was soon full of our musky smell, my lips raw from his stubble and salty skin. He pulled me deeper inside him but kept me moving and struggling to keep him pinned and still. He came with a roar that shook the mattress and shuddered through my body, and he wouldn't let me stop till I had emptied myself inside him. I collapsed onto the bed and he held me from behind, whispering in my ear that he was ready to see if I could make him do it a second time.

It was late when I dressed and let myself out of his apartment, taking with me the unfinished joint and another one that I plucked from his hiding spot (along with the stash I had bought from him earlier that night at the club). I thought about trying to flag down a ride back to The Legacy to get my car, but the damp air felt good in my lungs and the thin light of morning was stretching over the tops of the trees. I walked back to my room near campus where I was greeted by the yapping Rodney and his elderly owner, whom I convinced that I was just getting out of bed and offered to make her a cup of coffee.

"Such a gentleman," she said, seeing right through me and cracking a smile. "You should still be in bed with your someone special, not doting on some cranky old widow and her miserable pooch."

I stayed away from the club for a few days, settling back into my studies and working a double shift at a grocery store for a guy who was always covering for me. But Doc's bedroom performance haunted me and I wanted a repeat match. I wanted to get to know him better, unravel his mysteries and convince the Sisters—particularly David and Peaches—that Doc was a decent guy and widely misunderstood. On the weekend, I was back at The Legacy, lingering in the hallway and catching up on gossip. As I retrace my steps now, I see that I *was* the gossip; worried faces were glancing over shoulders or up from mirrors as Doc made his way over to speak to me. "Hey there, stranger," he said and pawed at my neck and shoulders. "I've got some stuff I think you might like."

During the performances, I followed Doc out to his car, where we sat and I allowed him to blow me. I didn't put up any struggle; in fact, I encouraged it and he rewarded *me* with a joint. "Don't be a stranger, kid," he said. "I always like showing off what I got and what I can do."

A few days later I found him sitting in his gray Mercedes in the parking lot of the flea market and reciprocated his attentions, beginning with a hand job and ending with me burying my head in his lap when the coast was clear of shoppers. (I'm not ashamed of my overt sexual behavior— I'd still do the same thing today given the same situation and players—but I am loathe to disclose that as part of my earning a joint, I "volunteered" to help Doc out with his business transactions, standing by the entrance of the flea market and whispering "Smoke? Smoke?" to any kind of deadhead, frat boy, or redneck that I could attract and steer toward Doc sitting in his car.)

After a couple of hours of this—it was a beautiful day and I considered my role more academic than criminal, something I could detail later in a class paper, perhaps— Doc gave me a wad of bills and told me to take off. I'd made more than four times the amount I could working the same amount of time at the grocery store. But hours later I was still calculating what my potential earnings would be if I followed through and became a regular drug dealer, and I had to shake myself awake to the rotten truth about the money—it was dishonest and a crime and nothing good would come of it.

I avoided both Doc and the club for a few more days, sampling drinks with R.J., the bartender at the Crystal Room of a midtown piano bar, and as the warmer weather arrived and classes headed into exams and papers due, I found my way to the tension-free locker rooms of the bathhouse.

One night, as I walked through the corridor of rooms, I noticed a familiar mop of hair, though I couldn't quite place him at first, and thinking it was someone I might need to avoid I turned abruptly away just as he looked at me and said, "Billy?" I recognized the voice, turned back and walked into the room and shut the door behind me. It was Austin, the pianist from *Hello, Dolly!* He was no longer wearing the eyeglasses he used when reading music, which accounted for the familiar but confusing appearance. He was reclining on the platform in the room, his towel covering his waist and upper thighs, and before he said anything else, I leaned in and kissed him to prevent him from starting a conversation and spoiling the attraction and the moment.

Austin Sawyer

Austin had a warm, furry kind of body, and as we groped and clutched each other, we would break away for a few seconds, smile and let our eyes meet. I knew he wanted to talk, but I felt that if we fell into a conversation first it was quite likely that nothing sexual would happen between us. His eyes said everything I wouldn't let him speak, however, and he seemed desperate to reach a quick orgasm, which I tempted and prolonged as much as I could.

Afterward, I stayed in the room for a long time, longer than I usually would linger when I hooked up with a stranger, and we relaxed into a spooning position.

"I had hoped something like this would happen during *Dolly*," he said. "I wanted to ask you out on a date. A real date."

I laughed and finished his thought, "But I wasn't ready for something like this." By now that young man seemed so far away from the one I had become. Austin confessed a lot about himself that night. He'd left Columbus to move to Atlanta and study piano. He talked about the first time he had sex with a guy—when he was eleven with his older cousin—and then how he had a boyfriend in high school who was now going to college in Arizona. He talked about how he wished he had learned to play the guitar instead of the piano, so he could be in a rock band, and then he talked about his job at the lounge in a downtown hotel—he wore a tuxedo and took requests for songs and had a champagne glass on the baby grand piano he played where people could leave tips. He loved performing. "I'd do it even if I didn't make money from it," he said, and I told him I understood what he meant—the theater had also had gotten into my blood. Somehow or other our conversation moved to Cliff's leaving and my growing friendship with David and soon Austin was explaining how he sometimes coached some of the lip-synchers who showed up for amateur night at The Legacy. "David often confuses beauty for talent," he said. "Some of these nelly boys he drags over for me to coach should just sing instead of lip—their voices are higher and more girly than Holly DeVine's." Then he told me that Holly was back in town and laying low, not letting Sabrina or Doc know she was back and working on a new set of songs.

"Doc's going to flip out when he hears this," I said.

"I've told her to be prepared for the worst, but she likes being oblivious. She won't even carry a can of mace."

"I don't think Doc would ever hurt her. *Seriously.*"

"What do you mean? He's already hurt her—black eye, broken ribs."

"She wants the attention," I said. "*His* attention. Doc can be a really great guy when she's not egging him on."

"Billy, he's a pusher and a bully. He'd pimp her out if he could get away with it. If she let him. And believe me he's tried."

"He's incredibly loyal to her."

"Loyal? He'd sell her off to the *lowest* bidder if there was something in it for him."

"You've got him all wrong," I said. "I've seen his good side. He's a lot of fun."

"*Fun?*"

After an acceptable beat, Austin began laughing, the kind of laughter that encouraged me to join in. I knew I didn't have to explain anything further. "Young man, you've accomplished something many of us have only fantasized about," he said. "How was it?"

"I'd do it again," I answered and smiled. "I *have* done it again."

"Have you slept with *her*?" Austin asked me next. "*Holly?*"

I was surprised by the question because the possibility or desire of having sex with Holly had never entered my mind. I had always considered Holly a real female and by doing so had instantly removed any kind of lust or desire to know her further. "Doc had a pretty strong hold on her," I answered and then explained that she was not what I was interested in experimenting with.

"We've played around a few times," Austin said.

I rolled my body over so that I was looking at him. His admission and his mischievous smile surprised me, so I asked how it was for him.

"Just what you'd expect," he said. "Soft. Easy. Not even as kinky as I hoped. More sweet than wild. I suppose I was hoping for more wild than sweet."

I smiled and nodded and imagined Doc and Holly having sex together and then tried to knock the image out of my mind by asking, "Do you think Holly's gonna go all the way? Have the operation? Get the change?"

"If she did, it would be a shame," Austin answered. "She has no problem using what she's got."

I've always justified that the events that followed and my participation in them were accidental. I harbored no motivation for the crimes, served as no catalyst for them, though they were nonetheless tragic and unfortunate for all of us involved. My guilt lies in my silence—not with preventing any of the events that happened, but preventing the crimes from being discovered and not telling the story until now. My memory wants to embellish these friends with humanizing details to provide more sympathy to our fates. I regarded Austin, for instance, as something of a self-made musical genius; he had studied piano since he was six, taking lessons at his church because his parents had not been able to afford a piano, and he was never impatient when rhythm failed others, always able to find a better way to teach it or to transpose the key of a song as easily as shifting the posture of his shoulders. Peaches was a community activist before it was *de rigueur*, petitioning the local business owners at the interchange of Cheshire Bridge and LaVista for better lighting and parking spots when the frat boys began harassing The Legacy patrons. (His first gay moment had been equally defiant: when an older boy threatened to beat him up if he did not suck his cock, Peaches beat him up and then offered him a blow job.) Lady Belle Lemmonds was also something of a pioneer. She had headlined Atlanta's first female impersonation show the cops didn't bust up, back in the early 1960s, at Mrs. P's, a small restaurant in the basement of the Ponce de Leon Hotel. She was often dodgy about her history prior to becoming Atlanta's high drag priestess, though on occasions she would admit to doing dress-up at age five in Jacksonville, a practice her mother had quickly tried to halt. She had owned an antique store on the Buckhead Strip since the Sixties, and after her success at Mrs. P's, she had headlined at the Sweet Gum Head, before taking the plunge and opening her own club. There were always rumors of Mafia backing and police payoffs at The Legacy—once, the police had broken up a fight by spraying tear gas. Peaches said that the wisest thing Lady Belle ever did was to rent the building, not try to own it, and thereby save herself numerous headaches because there was always something at the club that needed more attention than the performers and guests. Every month she sent a check to Henry and Miriam Sussman in Tarpon Springs, Florida, with her lip prints on it. And Sabrina Flair was more than just an impersonator; her skill as a seamstress for creating one-of-a-kind costumes for the hard-to-dress, broad-shouldered, full-figured gals at the Legacy also landed her commissions to design gowns for Atlanta's teenage society debutantes who wanted to look sparkly and fun. ("Every girl's gotta have a skill to fall back on, Sweetie," she would console some of the losing ladies who showed up for amateur night, "And I'm not talking about falling onto your back.") Holly, too, was not as fragile as I have portrayed her to be—she was a tough businesswoman about her image and reputation; in fact, she set an sequence of events into motion when she decided to return to the stage—and not with a new song at The Legacy, but with a bolder step up. She wanted to be a legitimate headliner. She wanted to perform a full-set act in the cabaret room at the Magic Garden, with Austin as her accompanist. No lip synching. Holly on her own.

Holly had returned to Atlanta, but had purposely slipped by Najarian's sharp radar detection; she was no longer living with her roommates on Juniper Street, instead sharing a studio apartment on West Peachtree with a waitress who worked day shifts at a restaurant at Phipps Plaza. Holly had approached Austin about the idea of doing a cabaret act, explaining how she wanted to give a theatrical setting to Marilyn Monroe's best songs, as if this were Marilyn's last concert or a retrospective of her career. Austin, because of his extensive musical contacts, knew a pianist who had played for another local act that had recently been booked in the cabaret room at the Magic Garden, and through him he convinced the owners of the club to give Holly's act a three-night weekend tryout. Najarian, now busy squiring and fighting with Sabrina, didn't get wind of Holly's cabaret aspirations until the gossip began backstage at Lady Belle's, when a sandwich board touting the upcoming

Michael B. Terrill
aka
Holly DeVine

show appeared one night outside the entrance of the Magic Garden. When Doc heard of the plan, jealousy and frustration set his rage into action.

Holly and Austin were both in the car when the first accident happened. Austin was pulling his red Mustang out of the parking lot of the Magic Garden when he was sideswiped. The car swerved over the curb and scraped against a utility pole, though neither he nor Holly, whom he was driving back to her apartment after a sound check rehearsal in the cabaret room, were hurt in any way other than being frightened and rattled. After Austin had inspected the damage to the side of the car and they had pulled back onto the road, Holly said that this sudden hit-and-run type of thing so late at night when there was little traffic on the road seemed suspicious, and she mentioned that she had been getting hang-up calls for the last day or so. She thought that Doc might have discovered where she was living. Austin dropped her off at her building—waiting to make sure she got into her apartment safely, leaving only after she waved to him from her screen door, and then he drove to a convenience store to get groceries before driving on to his apartment.

Austin was not so lucky. He was attacked from behind in the covered parking garage of his apartment building. As he was opening the trunk to get the paper bags, something cracked against his skull. I heard several accounts of what might have struck him—a car jack, a baseball bat, a hammer—whatever it was, he was thrown to the ground and not discovered until hours later. It was not until several days had passed, when I had heard through David that Holly's show had been canceled, that I also heard that Austin was in the hospital.

Austin required forty-seven stitches and did not regain consciousness until thirteen hours after being admitted to the hospital. I remember the cold walk of fear I felt when I showed up at the hospital and looked for his room, worried that that he might not remember who I was, his memories lost, his brain damaged. Peaches had told me of the attack. While Austin's injuries were not fatal or debilitating, they were the kind that would haunt him for the rest of his life—difficulty with the speed of his speech, headaches, an aversion to bright light. He had not seen his attacker, though when word of the attack reached backstage at The Legacy, it was believed that Najarian had either done it himself or arranged to have it done. Holly and Austin's sexual past was no more secret than Holly and Najarian's battles had been, so it was easy to link one misbehavior with the other. And the gray Mercedes that Doc drove around town now had long, treadlike scrapes of red paint along one side, though Doc told Peaches one night at the club it was the result of passing too close to a drive-thru bank teller's window.

Holly's show at the Magic Garden (or the Tragic Gardenia as it was soon nicknamed) was canceled—no pianist could learn Austin's complex arrangements on such a short notice. Holly, without any backup survival skill of her own, convinced Lady Belle to let her return to the lineup of The Legacy the following weekend. Lady Belle agreed, but only on the condition that Doc would not make any trouble. Or that Holly would not make any trouble for Najarian.

Things did not go well on Holly's first night back at the club. Najarian was there and he was intent on provoking a fight with her, claiming Holly was hurting him, making him miserable, blaming everything on him when he was just as innocent as she was. Their voices were loud and interrupting the performances. Lady Belle, on hand to keep things quiet, made Holly stay backstage and had Najarian leave the club, but Doc went no farther than out into the back parking lot, nursing a bottle of bourbon he kept in his Mercedes and smoking one cigarette after another until the shows were done for the evening.

I had spent some time at the baths that evening, then drove over to the club to find David to see if he wanted to go out to eat after his shows. (I was avoiding Doc myself, taking to heart another serious "talking to" Peaches had given me about living in the gutter. "Dearest," he had said, "it's one thing to be a tourist or a frequent guest of that exotic no-good-will-come-of-it place, but the moment you start believing that you belong there is the moment you're in trouble.") David was not interested in gossiping with me or even gauging the hyperactivity of Doc and Holly as long as they weren't interrupting LaVilla's big number; instead, David, or rather, LaVilla was flirting with a Georgia Tech senior whom he was convinced he could follow through with later that night. I watched some of the acts I had not seen before, then talked to Peaches for a while backstage. We agreed to eat at the Dunk 'N Dine after the shows and I had planned to meet Peaches in the parking lot behind The Legacy.

Peaches was always one of the last ones to leave the building; he took it as his duty to make sure that the lights were turned off, the bar was locked down, the stage-door Johnnies had either been paired off or left, and Lady Belle was not too drunk to lock the front and back doors of the club. That night Holly and Sabrina had lingered longer than usual, both hoping to avoid a confrontation with Doc in the parking lot. Holly had even asked Peaches to walk with her to her car, but both had been distracted by others. I was waiting outside by my car at the opposite end of the parking lot from where Najarian was waiting and drinking from his liquor bottle, annoyed by the delays everyone's sensitivities seemed to be causing that night. At this point I was hungry and anxious to leave, still buzzing from some kind of upper a trick at the baths had slipped me earlier in the evening and the beer I'd had while watching the acts inside the club. And my own vanity was wounded. I was crushed that Doc was ignoring me as determinedly as I was ignoring him. Earlier, he had given me a blank stare when he should have said hello, not because he didn't want to acknowledge me, or so I have always thought, but because he was consumed by a rage of jealousy over Holly and couldn't see his way past that.

Holly came out the back door first, without Peaches. Najarian sprinted toward her. In two or three steps, he was pulling her toward his car, saying, "Baby, Baby, *I'll* make you a star," the bourbon bottle dangling from his other hand. Holly was only feebly resisting, as if she wasn't sure she wanted to protest or not. Sabrina exited the back door next, saw Doc and Holly struggling, and ran toward them to break it up. There was a strange, momentary dance as the three of them circled each other, Doc grasping Holly, Sabrina grasping Doc. Because of the drugs and my hunger, my reflexes were slow. I started across the parking lot to see about breaking things up when their little circle was split apart. Sabrina had been tugging at Doc's jacket sleeve and somehow ended up grasping the bourbon bottle instead. In a flash she had crashed it against the side of Najarian's head.

The bottle didn't break, just sounded a deep *whack* as it landed against the bone of his skull. Doc dropped his hold of Holly's hand and fell to his knees, his mouth and eyes wide with pain, which gave Holly enough freedom and space to take a step and kick him in the stomach. Then she grabbed the bottle from Sabrina and hit Najarian again at the side of his head. Peaches, coming out of the back door now, only saw Doc drop further to the ground, his head landing with a soft *thumpf* on the dark cement. Peaches reached them a few seconds after I had, leaning down and checking Najarian's breathing.

"He's not breathing," Peaches said.

A small pool of dark liquid had gathered in Najarian's ear. *Blood.* "What did you do?" Peaches asked, looking up at Holly and Sabrina.

Holly, still holding the bourbon bottle and looking down at Doc, let the bottle slip from her hand and it shattered when it hit the pavement. "Is he dead?" she asked, in her girlish whisper.

Peaches, kneeling down and opening Doc's mouth with his fingers and then pressing them against his neck, answered, "There's no pulse. I can't find a pulse." He rolled Doc over so that he lay on his back, pressed his lips against Doc's mouth and blew air into his body, pumping his hands against Doc's unresponsive chest. We watched this exercise at resuscitation as if it were another performance. Color was drained from everything around us—the black, humid night soaking in the street lamps and leaving only a grizzly pale haze. Peaches stood up and the four of us became another strange little circle that evening, looking down at Doc's lifeless body. I know it occurred to Peaches that we were in trouble, big trouble, because it occurred to me at that same moment and I was a sluggish mess. I'd always considered Peaches to be the sharpest tack in the little hut of Lady Belle's Legacy and everyone was waiting for him to tell the rest of his Little Sisters what to do.

And then a sound from behind disturbed all of us; the back door of the club was being opened and closed. We turned to see who it was.

It was Lady Belle, leaving for the night, fumbling with her keys as she tried to lock the door.

"Need any help?" I yelled over to her and walked away from the group, hoping to distract Lady Belle from the scene. Lady Belle was drunk, but she managed to lock the door, and I walked with her to where her car was parked, fortunately not far from my own at the other end of the lot, where employees were encouraged to park their cars, leaving the ones closer to the building available for paying clients and patrons.

"Can you drive okay?" I asked her as she searched through her keys for the one to unlock her car door.

She looked up at me, annoyed and flattered, and said, "This is nothing, ya sexy thang, you. Piece of cake."

She unveiled the car key slowly, taking a great deal of effort—or showmanship—to unlock the door and lower herself into the driver's seat. She was dressed as most of the drag queens were when they left the club, in jeans and a T-shirt, still wearing full warpaint and her skull covered with a baseball cap. I wanted to offer to drive her home—it would have been a viable escape hatch—but I waited near her car as she started the engine, backed out of the space and drove out into the street, all without noticing the small group of nervous drag queens who remained behind on the other side of the parking lot.

As I've replayed these events in my mind in the intervening years, I've always imagined that this was when Najarian died, while I was across the lot helping Lady Belle and keeping her from becoming involved, but watching her drive away, too drunk to be behind the wheel of a car. What had been a comic and unusual scenario as I had approached the fighting and tugging, now seemed catastrophic and surreal when I returned to the group—they had all been watching Lady Belle drive away, hoping, I sensed, that somehow she would magically carry all of us from this moment because she was our guiding and protective spirit.

Then Peaches said, "Put him in his car."

None of us moved from where we were standing so he said, again, more forcefully, "Help me put him in his car."

Holly and Sabrina backed off, stepping farther away from Najarian's slumped body at the same time as if were part of a choreographed routine.

I searched out Peaches' eyes, just as he had on the night we first met. "Are you sure we should do this?" I asked him.

"Yes," he nodded.

Peaches and I lifted Doc from the ground and dragged his body awkwardly by his hands and feet across the parking lot and leaned him against his Mercedes.

"We have to get a plan together, girls," Peaches said, turning to Holly and Sabrina. "Who has his keys?"

"Check his pockets," Holly said, dabbing away her tears.

Peaches rolled his eyes in her most theatrical, disgusted manner and plunged a hand into Najarian's pants pocket. The keys weren't there, and he checked the other side, and when he didn't find them there, either, he found them in Doc's inside jacket pocket. Peaches unlocked the car door and then tossed me the keys, saying, "Let's put him in the trunk."

"The trunk?" Holly wailed. "You can't put Doc in the trunk!"

"You think he can drive his car?" Peaches shot back. "You have a better idea?"

I unlocked the trunk. Peaches tilted Doc's body and held him up by the neck and began to try to pull his jacket off. It was an impossible struggle and he looked at Holly and said harshly, "Well, help me!"

Holly only took a step backwards and folded her arms across her chest, her face turning into a silent scream. I moved closer and helped Peaches with the jacket. When we had twisted it off Doc's body, Peaches wrapped it around Doc's head, covering his scalp and face.

"You can't do that!" Holly cried.

"You have a better idea?" Peaches answered, and then looked over at Sabrina and said, "You? Can't you help?"

Sabrina shook her head and stepped beside Holly, cowering behind her.

I lifted Doc's feet and Peaches held him at his shoulders and we shuffled a few feet and swung him into the trunk of his car. I had no idea what kind of trouble I had already stepped into and like Sabrina and Holly I was looking to Peaches on what would happen next.

I slammed the trunk shut and Peaches turned to where Holly and Sabrina were still standing motionless and frightened. "We're going to the Dunk 'n Dine. All of us. *Together*. Sabrina, you ride with Billy. Holly, you come with me."

"I'm not hungry," Holly said.

"Doesn't matter," Peaches said. "You need an alibi. We all need an alibi. And it needs to be the same one."

"I just want to go home," Sabrina said.

"Unfortunately, you left home without your ruby slippers," Peaches answered. "So you're gonna have to spend some time with the rest of us. Now keep quiet and get into Billy's car. The sooner we get there the safer we're all gonna be."

It was a short drive to the Dunk 'n Dine, almost across the street, but enough time for Sabrina to sniffle, cry, and moan, "None of this is my fault." I didn't offer her any compassion, nor did I remind her that she threw the first swing. I knew I was in already over my head and was worried myself about potential repercussions.

Holly and Peaches were already seated when Sabrina and I joined them at a booth. We didn't have a moment to commiserate because Bobby Ray was already at the table, greeting us and handing out menus, asking how the crowd at the club was that night.

Peaches went into full performance mode, explaining there was a rowdy group of dykes at the Legacy that evening. "Mind you, I don't have anything against them," he said. "But they've got their own inside jokes and they throw the timing off of everything."

"Fruit loops in flannel," Bobby Ray answered. "Table of them just left."

When Bobby Ray sauntered away, I knew our alibi had been established, but Sabrina and Holly remained aloof and unsociable, petulant because they had not been allowed to run away and hide. I had grown quiet myself, lost in replaying the sequence of Doc's last moments in the parking lot and wanting to desperately confide my participation in the events with someone.

When Bobby Ray reappeared to take our food orders, we looked at him as if we had forgotten where we were. But Peaches again picked up the slack, prodding us for choices until we had all chosen something from the menu.

"Heard Austin Sawyer got banged up a bit," Bobby Ray said, looking at Holly. "How's he doing?"

Holly eyes widened and she dramatically placed her fingers against her cheeks. "It wasn't my fault," she said. "I had nothing to do with it."

"No one said you did, Darlin'," Peaches answered, patting Holly's hand. "Tough night at the club," he added, rolling his wide eyes in a circle. "Real fish, you know?"

"I hear ya," Bobby Ray said and walked away from the table.

I would rank that meal together as one of my most awkward experiences. Once Holly broke into tears, she never stopped crying. She never tasted the omelet that Peaches had coaxed her to order, and left the rest of us so uneasy we only moved the food on our plates from one side to the other.

"Listen up," Peaches said, shaking Holly's arm to keep her quiet. "We all have to stick together on this. Nothing happened tonight in the parking lot. We all met after the show, came here for food. Got it?"

"You never knew him like I did," Holly sobbed.

"On the contrary, Darlin'," Peaches answered. "All of us knew him. Each of us had a special piece of him, ain't that right, Billy?"

"What?" Holly asked.

"You heard me. Doc loved to share his special gift with anyone who wanted to sample it. I tasted it one night about a year ago. It's a cryin' shame he wasn't the sort of man his dick was."

Holly scrunched up her face in disgust and pushed her way out of the booth, but before she left the table she made sure she had delivered her own devastating line. "This isn't about sex," she said. "It's about the man I loved."

"Sabrina, go check up on her," Peaches said.

"Me?"

"You're the only one of us who could pass in the ladies' room."

"I'll take that as a compliment," she said and scooted her way out of the booth.

Peaches watched her dramatically sashay down the aisle, as if she were a fashion model on a runway, then he turned to me and said, "I have an idea. I'll drop these two off. Wait for me outside my apartment building."

I nodded and gave Peaches a worried look. In a beat he realized the gravity of the situation and his request and added, "You'll help, right?"

"Of course," I answered. And for me, too, this was more than sex.

Peaches' plan was to drive Doc's car to a remote area, far away from downtown Atlanta, remove the license plate, hide and abandon both the body and the car. "Preferably some place in Alabama," he said. "And somewhere before daylight."

"Shouldn't we just report it to the police?" I asked. "Tell them the truth?"

"The truth would hurt us more," he answered. "The police will search the car and find our fingerprints. Then they will search the club and our apartments and find out all sorts of sordid little facts and details about our lives which will become public knowledge, not to mention that they will charge every single one of us with a bunch of crimes. Manslaughter. Murder. Sodomy. Any of us talk to the police, we all go straight to jail. And we'll be there the rest of our lives."

I could have forced the issue. I could have reported the crime. Or I could have walked away, pretended none of it had happened. But it did. And whatever I did or didn't do from that moment on, I would mark myself as a criminal, whether the fact of it would remain private or become public.

It was late when I picked Peaches up at his apartment building and we drove to the parking lot behind the Legacy. I had suggested a place upstate where I thought we could conceal Doc's Mercedes, about two hours' drive from Atlanta. Peaches would follow me in Doc's car.

We avoided driving along the Interstate, and if there was any luck to be had that evening, we found it by avoiding the stopgap of red lights. Normally I would have listened to the radio to speed along the trip, but instead I felt it more appropriate to remain quiet and contemplative. I thought about a lot on that drive, how my life had changed so quickly in less than a year. I wondered if I had made the right choices thus far, what changes I should make once we had completed this task.

When I reached the route to the lake, I signaled for Peaches to follow. A few minutes later we had parked near a steep ravine.

Peaches went right to work, removing the license plate from the rear end of the car. By morning we were done, back on the highway and on the outskirts of Atlanta.

I've always explained that the reason why I left the South and moved to Manhattan was that I wanted to live out and openly, away from the discrimination and shame my family would have directed at me if I had remained in Atlanta and come out to them as homosexual. But that statement is only partially true; I also left the South because I was scared and ashamed about what had happened that night in the parking lot of The Legacy and I was afraid that I would be hunted down and avenged in the name of justice, just as the Watergate criminals had been.

In the days following Doc's death, I stayed mostly in bed, skipping classes and drinking myself into an intoxicated exhaustion. Holly left town again, hiding out at her cousin's place in Roswell. Sabrina went with Chanelle Tempest to perform in Mobile. Peaches carried on as if nothing out of the ordinary had happened, writing down new jokes and routines to perform at The Legacy. In a rare twist of fate, Lady Belle's shuttered for good a month later because of "financial mismanagement," though the story I heard was it had something to do with health inspectors and the "tiny appetizers" Lady Belle had added to the menu, but another version claimed that the bar's liquor license had been revoked "after police caught a customer getting a blow job in the bathroom." One by one the Spectacular Sisters who had played The Unforgettable Hideaway began to drift up the street to the stage of the Sweet Gum Head, now offering the best drag show in town.

It could have all played out differently. I've done the "what if" game countless times over the years. To my knowledge there was no investigation done with Najarian's disappearance—it was as if he were the true criminal, absconding, on the lam, in hiding—the ruin of others.

For a long time afterward, I knew it rankled David that I knew something about the way Najarian disappeared that he didn't know; first, he never cared about it, then, when he did, he was annoyed that no one offered him an explanation and he took this as a clue that all was not as it seemed to be, and for a while I knew he held it against me, using a silent treatment toward me in retaliation for my secret. I lived the next few weeks in an abyss of fear and despair. I wandered around campus crazed with grief and sorrow and disbelief, oblivious to my whereabouts. I'd never grieved over anything or anyone before and it pained me whenever someone tried to engage me in conversation. I felt so dishonest and sinful. I holed up for hours in my bedroom drinking, till I stumbled to the kitchen to wash out a glass, frightening my landlady because she had thought she was in the house alone and sending a startled Rodney on a yapping spree that didn't let up until I disappeared from his sight.

I'd always believed that there would be more visible repercussions from Najarian's death: A blackmail letter. A threat of retaliation. But the truth was that the aftershocks of Najarian's death, or murder, or cover-up, or crime, however you name it, diminished and changed all of my relationships in town, or at least the way I viewed them. It began, once again, with Cliff. It was now the end of the spring semester and I was barely passing my courses; every failing moment I was convincing myself that these would be my last days in school, that I would tell my parents I would not be returning in the fall, and that I wanted to move to New York and find a job in the professional theater. It sounded like a foolish course. But I wanted to run away. I wanted to change myself into someone else. One day as I was rushing to the library on some errand I ran into Cliff; ever since he had returned to school after his father's death, he had kept to himself, and, at times, it made me think that he was purposely avoiding me. He was. From what I knew, he knew nothing of Najarian's disappearance because he was hardly aware of him, and as much as I wanted to share the details with him, I kept my promise to Peaches to keep it all a secret. When I stopped on the path that circled the

Administration Building to say hello to Cliff and ask how he was and see if he wanted to get together as soon as exams were done, he said bluntly, "I can't see you anymore, Billy."

"What do you mean?" I asked. My heart was crashing against my ribs. I thought he knew about what had happened to Doc.

"I'm not gay anymore," he said. "It's a sin. It's a crime. We could go to jail for what we do. I could get fired from a job if it was discovered. And I don't want to spend the rest of my life in hell."

That was the moment I decided to leave Atlanta, the third kick in the heart—Austin's injury, Doc's death, Cliff's walking away from me as if I were an irredeemable sinner. The one person who might have gotten me to stay in Atlanta had served, instead, as the catalyst for my escape. His rejection of me—and the life he had opened up for me—went to the marrow of my bones. I was only a "phase" and a "mistake" to him. I did not wait until the fall to move; instead, I packed a duffel bag a week after final exams and boarded a train to New York City, arriving a day later with only a list of addresses of places that might accept me as the person I wanted to be.

Those first few months in New York were as hard as the ones I had just spent in Atlanta. I was alone and I struggled with whether I was abandoned or had abandoned my friends. But my ambition distracted and protected me. I went to all sorts of classes—dance, acting, voice—finding new teachers and mentors and another group of friends and "sisters" and "brothers."

Over the years, news came to me of my former friends in Atlanta and at the Legacy, either through their visits to New York or when I was back in Georgia to see my family for a holiday visit. Austin became a band instructor at a high school in the northern suburbs, taking his marching band to state finals four years in a row before transferring to another school in Alabama. Holly moved to Switzerland, continued her hormones and injections, and then had a sex change; I heard that she worked in clubs in Hollywood before moving permanently to Germany, and that the less and less she looked like Marilyn, the more exotic her speech and voice became, until she had acquired a thick accent as if she had never spoken English. Sabrina continued impersonating Judy and Liza and Barbra and made a decent living on the gay club circuit—Palm Springs, Provincetown, Seattle, New Orleans. Once, my lover Sean and I caught her act when she was performing at a new club in the West Village that was promoting "dinner and drag shows," and we had drinks together after her performance. While Sean was chatting up a handsome waiter, I took the opportunity to ask Sabrina if she ever thought about Doc.

"Doc? I wonder what became of him," she answered and held a faraway gaze in her eyes. "He just disappeared one day. Like so many...good men."

I nodded and didn't pursue the memory any further; Sabrina, I assumed, had constructed her own rationale to survive, like we all did. In her mind, Doc had merely moved away. That bourbon bottle had never been grasped and swung with an angry effort.

Peaches became quite the activist. In 1986, three days after the Supreme Court's decision in *Bowers v. Hardwick*, he helped gather two hundred protesters outside the Russell federal building on Spring Street. He was one of the organizing forces behind the Atlanta chapter of ACT UP, but his own illness prevented him from traveling out of town for many national demos. I had heard he was ill when he moved in with David. David nursed and babied him in his final days. David died about a year later, writing me notes and leaving me messages on my answering machine telling me that Peaches, in his final hours, had spilled the true story to him of what had happened that night in the parking lot of the Legacy. And then, as more years passed, and I settled into a relationship and was also unsettled by my own illness, I began to remember pieces of things I had thought I had forgotten or purposely avoided, like the way Doc's body smelled that night he died, a pasty, sweet metallic smell, as blood swelled his face and booze seeped through his skin.

It is time for me to account for my own behavior, to confess my guilt and desire for self-preservation. All this happened years ago when I was young and I had everything ahead of me, everything except what a crime could stop cold. This was the reason why I behaved the way I did—why I left town and why I so seldom looked behind me anymore. But I also did it to protect my friendships. My year in Atlanta had made me stronger and more determined to succeed. My Sisters had taught me well. "Chin up and tits out," Peaches always preached. "You can flub a line and still get a laugh. But never, Honey Bunch, never, ever, under any circumstances, let anyone see you sweat. No one likes a sorry drag queen."

William B. Goodman
aka
Billy Graham

William B. Goodman was born William Ray Graham on December 14, 1955, in Galena, Georgia. He graduated in 1973 from Galena High School and attended Rabun College on an academic scholarship. The following year he transferred to Candler College in Atlanta, but after only a year of study, he moved to New York City, where he worked a number of odd jobs before landing a part in the chorus of *The Grand Tour*, a musical starring Joel Grey, and changing his professional surname to Goodman to avoid any confusion with the popular evangelist. Goodman appeared in a number of small parts off-Broadway before writing and starring in *The Augmented Third*, about the overlapping relationships within a group of touring musicians. In the mid-1980s, Goodman began more serious writing about AIDS, including the play *By Another Name*, one of the earliest works to deal with AIDS discrimination, and the novel, *A Gentle Way*, about the relationship between an AIDS patient and his volunteer caregiver. Later in the decade, Mr. Goodman became an important force in the activist groups ACT UP and Queer Nation, abandoning writing for more than five years while he was a member of the Treatment and Data group focusing on the establishment of parallel track trials for the establishment of new AIDS drugs. His nonfiction account of this work, including his own body's unresponsiveness to the new drug cocktails to combat the HIV virus, was published in 1996 as *The Inexplicable Chain*. Goodman died at his home in Manhattan in 1998 of complications from AIDS. He was forty-two.

The following reproductions are provided from the personal papers of Sean Burke and are reprinted by permission of Mr. Burke and the family of Paul Ramsey.

Sabrina Flair

May 4, 1998

Dear Sean,

    I was heartbroken to read about Billy yesterday.
I saw an item in a gossip column in Pink, a bar rag
that is dropped off at Rendezvous, the club where I
am performing in Minneapolis this month. I am deeply
sorry for your loss—our loss. Billy was always a
true gentleman in everything he did—I know, we
shared many secrets and scandals in our younger
days in Atlanta and I am grateful for his help and
respect during a particularly rough time in our
past.
    A reporter from The Advocate once asked me
to comment about my history and close friendship
with Billy and I was very vague—well, Billy and I
were both vague about things between us, actually,
because there was always a very incriminating
story that he could have told and never did to
my knowledge. I'm sending you this page from my
diary—it was written the night I last saw you
and Billy at Babe's in the Village. Billy whispered

something to me that unsettled me because it was so deeply hidden in our past by both of us—and I had to go home and write about it and I realized when I put it all down that I had wanted to tell him something too and hadn't gotten the chance, because I had been so distracted by what he had brought up. I meant to write him about it but forgot to do that too.

I've been dedicating songs in memory of Billy in my act this last week. He always came to see me perform whenever we were in the same city at the same time, and he loved that old Garland chestnut that I do from A Star is Born—"The Man That Got Away"—which I think is a fitting tribute to him.

All my best in this time of sorrow,

With much love,

Sabrina Flair

February 10, 1997

Dear Diary,

   Well, another night of performances at Babe's
is finally over! Only 16 more to go. I can't wait until
this awful contract expires and I can get back out
on the road and be somewhere else other than this
horrid dump. I never understand why people love
Manhattan so much—there is too much traffic,
too many people, and waaay too much attitude—
and anyone and everyone has an opinion on what
you should do and how you should do it, instead of
minding their own business and trying to do their
own lousy job. I can't even read any of the reviews
from this lousy gig because they all mention that
Judy was never, never EVER this overweight! If they
only knew what I had to put up with! This apartment
I am subletting in Hell's Kitchen (name apropos) is no
bigger than my shoe closet in Tallahassee and there
is always something not right about it every minute
of every day—no hot water, no fuse box, no heat,
too much heat, the window won't open, the door
won't lock, and on and on. And the clubs in this city
are even worse—I don't understand how they get
away with half the stuff they do here—there is no
stage to speak of at Babe's—we perform BETWEEN
TABLES—or sometimes stand on a box no bigger (or
safer) than a crate. Tonight there was a mouse in

the main dining room and it was running from table to table and making me crazy, crazy, crazy! I kept looking at my feet all night long while I was singing, like I was some kind of amateur or something! I mean, I have performed in plenty of dumps, but this one takes the cake!

Billy Goodman and his hunky boyfriend were at the show tonight along with two friends of his— Jameson Currier and his friend John Doyle, whom I've also met a couple of times before. Billy looked too thin to me but he is as handsome as ever (particularly with that wash of gray going through his hair now). I didn't really get a chance to check up on him and his health in detail—though I know most of the messy stuff because of what he has written about it—I read that new book of his from cover to cover when it came out. I sat with him and his friends at their table for a few minutes after the show. (And told them about the mouse in the house and made them all check their feet!)

I was about to tell Billy a story about when I was performing in a small club in Norfolk, when he leaned in and asked me something about Doc. Yaman Najarian. Did I ever think about Doc anymore? I evaded his question, of course, even though his lover and friends were yacking with one of the waiters about something or other and not paying any attention to us. (They were talking with Moji, the gorgeous stud from Lebanon.) Just the mention of

Doc's name sent me into shock—our friend Peaches, bless her lost soul, beat it into my head to never, never, EVER, mention anything about him, which was my initial reflex when Billy brought up Doc's name. I think about Doc a lot—it was a shame and a crime what happened to him, though it wasn't my fault—it was because of another lousy two-bit street bitch who thought she could sing. And I won't let my rage take me there tonight.

Anyway, I felt so bad lying to Billy that I didn't know who he was talking about, when he knew the whole damned story! And I feel so bad that I didn't get to tell him about Norfolk because he made me forget! Hopefully, I will remember to write him about it—or call him—or tell him the next time I see him, because it was about Cliff Jackson, the guy he was head over heels for in Atlanta years ago. Cliff showed up at one of my performances in Norfolk and we had a nice, long chat—or a drunken ramble, depending on your point of view. There was hardly anyone else at the show—the cabaret room was above a disco, and most of the guys were there to dance, not to listen to me sing. (God, they were all so young—one twinkie who chatted me up didn't even know who Garland was!!!)

So Cliff unraveled his own rocky trail (my god, don't we all have 'em): he got married, had two kids, got divorced when his wife found out he was having gay flings on the side, and then his ex-wife took him to the cleaners—most of his money going to alimony and child support. He looked pretty good—heavier and beefier than the old days—like the money he hadn't spent on his wife and kids had been spent on plenty of good food and expensive booze. He turned into a sorta messy drinker (though I matched him glass for glass). Somewhere during our fourth drink, he brought up the subject of Billy Graham—now Billy Goodman—and literally started bawling because he said he had let the opportunity of having a relationship with Billy just slip through his fingers. He was full of regret, literally wailing, "I shouldn't have brushed him off," and "I shouldn't have told him I didn't want to see him anymore." I asked him if he felt this way because Billy was now baby famous, and he looked at me with his big ole teary eyes and said, "I guess you never slept with him, then—."

Hmmmm, that got me. So I asked him, what did he mean? Was Billy a "big boy?" (Meaning his endowment—)

He said Billy was not only a "big boy," but he was in the top three best fucks of his lifetime (thankfully, he didn't elaborate on the other two, or if he did, I was too smashed to remember them.) He said that Billy had more passion in his little fingers than most guys have in their entire bodies. I always thought that about Billy, too. You always knew what he thought and where you stood with him. But then Cliff said something very interesting—he said that he had given Billy his name, that the night they first spent together, he had complimented Billy on being a "good man." And it was always a running joke between them—they needed to find a "good man" to have some fun with. Silly boys, if you ask me—they don't know a good thing when they've got one.

Anyway, I had wanted to tell Billy that he had a reputation beyond all them brilliant words he writes and that Cliff had never, never, EVER forgotten him and that now I knew the true secret behind his nom de plume I certainly wouldn't spill them beans either, but I forgot because I was thinking again about Doc.

Before I left the club tonight, I told Moji about the mouse-in-the-house and he said that I should report it to the Health Department, so I have just spent the last HOUR looking through the hugely thick Manhattan yellow pages trying to find the right phone number to call tomorrow morning to report that scumbag of a man I am working for so that the city of New York will close down that lousy sweat shop and I can leave and find a better gig.

That's all for tonight.

More drama tomorrow.

The following is a printed version of a widely distributed email obtained through one of the recipients who has requested anonymity. It is reprinted as the archive of a public statement and not as private correspondence. All legal inquiries should be directed to the attention of the publisher of this edition.

From: divineone@hollydivine.com
To: FI@list.com, calendar@eurocabaret.org,
QFdistribution@hollydivine.com
Date: 01/14/03 12:49:07 a.m.
Re: My Posterity

To all my dearest fans and closest friends,
please accept my apologies for this e-mail but
haste makes me write to all of you to clarify
many things which have come to my immediate
attention. I am both appalled and flattered to
be informed that parts of my persona were used
by the late William B. Goodman in his fictional
story about the deplorable circumstances
befalling the boyfriend of a certain drag
queen. I have only recently been told that
Billy's last boyfriend allowed this story to
be published to help settle the expenses of
Billy's long and unfortunate illness. But
Dear Ones, let me use this moment to explain
to all of you sweet things that I am in
no way the character that is portrayed in
that story. Please note the spelling. Holly
diVine is not Holly DeVine. And neither one
ever had a boyfriend named Dr. Yaman Najarian
in Atlanta or any other town in the United
States or abroad. As far as I know, Dr. Yaman
Najarian never existed—he is truly a figment
of a writer's fanciful imagination.

Yes, I will admit to one and all that
Billy Goodman née Graham and I were friends
many years ago and I do remember him as a
beautiful young boy who visited us backstage
at the great and sorely missed Unforgettable

Hideaway, the fabulous Lady Belle's Legacy club in Atlanta, GA. And yes, I was also good friends with LaVilla Débris and Miss Sincerely Peaches, though not as good a friend with Sabrina Flair, though we have worked together peacefully and professionally on many of the same stages without any of the animosities or jealousies that Mr. Goodman would lead you to believe existed in his fictional tale.

There are some other points that this writer raises in his not-true story that I also want to clarify and explain for you while I have your attention. Let me be very clear—I do not lip synch and I was never a lip syncher. I am an entertainer who performs live before an audience. And I have never, ever, in my entire wonderful and beautiful career, considered myself simply a Marilyn impersonator (though I do do a terrific Marilyn number in my act). I like to consider myself a true blend of the best artists of all time—my humor is "Lucy," my looks "Lana," and my voice now more "Marlene" than "Marilyn." (Yes, Dearest Ones, my voice is lower than it was years before, and I attribute that to living a good life in and out of the pink and blue spotlights, and as for my accent, which Mr. Goodman rudely insults as fake and foreign, it is the true and honest way I speak after living for many years on the European continent.)

Please let me also state that I never had a cousin who lived in the lovely town of Roswell in northern Georgia nor have I ever been to that fine and decent place in that good and blessed state. I was born in Arkansas and raised in Florida, Dear Ones, and let me emphatically explain that I never thought I was going to become a performer at the legendary Jewel Box Revue in Palm Beach, which was where my own legacy began. This is one of the most important facts which Mr. Goodman unfortunately omitted in his story, if he was, indeed, trying to summon up my true character and personality. At my audition for that fabulous show I thought I was being hired as a male dancer, but my first night on the job with the Revue, the stage manager asked me where my wig and makeup was—I was expected to be dressed and on stage in less than a half-hour. And this is how it all came to be. How I came to be on the stage and performing in front of the world as I know it.

Since I was, first and foremost, a Jewel Box veteran performer, this was how I was booked to perform a special solo act at the Magic Garden cabaret in Atlanta. (It was not canceled as Billy stated in this fictional and not-true story because a jealous boyfriend mugged the pianist.) I did, however, find some true and loving experiences amongst a member of my audience which made me want to linger longer than usual in Atlanta before hitting the other great cities and infamous clubs on the great FI cabaret circuit, and this was how I came to headline for a while at Lady Belle's Legacy and got to know Billy. Lady Belle knew and respected me and had seen my performances and wanted me for her club. And as for this "interest" which kept me in Atlanta, my man did not die by a blow to the head from a bourbon bottle, nor did he mysteriously disappear. He lived in one of those lovely, upscale homes in the pricey Virginia-Highlands neighborhood and had no connection with Billy's so called "gay underworld."

Billy also left out many of the highlights of my wonderful and fabulous career to date. While I was in Southern California, I won the titles International Show Queen, Queen of the Universe, and Miss California Continental. After my wonderful year touring the great western states with that last title, I decided to tour the whole country, or as much of it as I could, which led to my bookings the following year on the luscious continent of Europe.

My legal name is not Michael B. Terrill, nor has it ever been Michael B. Terrill at any time in my life. And as far as my sexual identity goes, I have always, since a child, wanted to face the world as a female. I was never interested in a male life. It was not who I wanted to be. I lived in the way I had to until I could reassign myself to a more female persona. I was, and am, an individual first—not a post-op anything. I am a woman now, but I don't try to hide my past or my history. And I am comfortable in my skin.

I have had a lot of highlights in my life and I hope they're not over yet. I like to make people laugh and smile and consider myself "Just a Little Girl from Little Rock," so everything that happened in my career has been a highlight for me. I did not know, being a simple person, that all these wonderful things would happen in my life, like performing at the wonderful "Carrousel de Paris" and having my own cabaret room in Hamburg or that I would be asked to perform for many of the royal heads of Europe and members of state from around the world.

And which leads me to write to you that after reading Mr. Goodman's fictional account of someone like me (but not me), I have started to put pen to paper myself and write my own memoirs. I have decided to tell my true story the way it must be told. I am already hard at work rectifying all the damage that has been done by someone other than myself. And what I won't leave out is the fabulous, divine truth. What it was like to be in front of an audience—singing, dancing—being just me.

XXXOOO,

Holly diVine

Sean Burke

AFTERWORD

Sean Burke

I have always been grateful for Jameson Currier's interest in Billy Goodman's account of his time in Atlanta that is detailed in *The Man That Got Away*, and his determination to help put together a consideration of the reasons why Billy abruptly decided to leave Georgia for New York before finishing a college degree.

As the story and bio goes, Billy lived in Atlanta for twelve months, from August, 1974 to July, 1975, but in that short space of time he became sexually and romantically involved with a male college friend and was introduced to Atlanta's underground gay community, particularly the dance and drag clubs along Cheshire Bridge Road. And, as Billy's narrative suggests, he was complicit in the cover-up of a crime—the murder of an Atlanta drug dealer who was a frequent patron of these same clubs.

Privately, Billy always admitted that the psychological toll of participating in the cover-up was the reason why he left Atlanta, though he notes that the months he spent in Atlanta were an educational and developmental process that was critical in shaping all facets of his older self.

Billy worked on the narrative account of this time, *The Man That Got Away*, for more than a decade, more determinedly after the deaths in the early 1990s of his friends Steve Parker (Sincerely Peaches) and David Duffy (LaVilla Débris), mostly fretting over how to keep the crime and its resulting cover-up from overshadowing the narratives of his coming out, his sexual awakening, and his new friendships, and without the camp and drag elements diminishing the impact of the crime (an accidental murder) and the secrets to keep it concealed. Billy always saw the cover-up as the bigger crime of the two, in part, because of his direct participation in it. As Billy's first reader, I read many versions of the story, watching it expand and contract, new characters added and old ones subtracted, while Billy's greatest concern that—as presenting the story as a nonfiction account—he (and we) could be subjected to lengthy inquiries and litigation if authorities were to look into the crimes it depicted. This concern also shaped the story-telling. In all versions that I read there was always something missing: Billy did not disclose the location of the hidden car and the missing body.

"Why would I write that?" he always answered. "And risk going to jail?"

And so the whereabouts of the car are both the mystery and the truth to this story. The narrative stops when Peaches and Billy reach a lake in north Georgia to dispose of the evidence.

At the beginning of May in 2014, I received an email from Billy's sister. After all of the arguments and threats and demands and counter demands from Billy's family in the first years after his passing in 1998 we had reached an unbalanced peace. I seldom now heard from one of his immediate relatives more than once a year, though there was always something further to discuss about the status of Billy's estate or the family's questions about the small non-profit foundation the estate funded. When I saw her name in my inbox, I felt certain that she was writing about the recent and successful revival of *The Augmented Third* that the Priority Theater in New York had mounted and that she was most likely inquiring again about the monetary rights she felt the family should receive. It had been widely reported that there was also interest in a movie adaptation with big Hollywood names. According to the court-settlement between the estate and the family, however, the family was not entitled to any proceeds of Billy's writings and the estate now donated all receipts and royalties earned from Billy's work to the foundation.

When I finally found the courage a few hours later to click open the message, I learned that Janet Barron, Billy's sister, was writing to let me know that Billy's mother had died a few months prior and that Janet and her husband were cleaning out her parents' house to sell the property. Janet was writing to inquire if I was interested in going through any of the boxes Billy had stored in the attic and basement before they were destroyed. As the beneficiary and executor of Billy's estate and the president of the foundation—hence the protracted legal battles—I hadn't been aware of any of Billy's belonging that remained stored at the house. I felt certain that if I were to express an interest in them there would be more legal bills involved, something I wanted to avoid. But it was also my duty as Billy's executor to retrieve the items and send anything of importance to the archive of his papers which was now housed in the Special Collections at the New York Public Library.

I also detected from the sense of urgency embedded in Janet's emails that she was also feeling out how litigious I and the estate might be with the further news she was supplying. The house where she and Billy had been born and grew up in was being demolished. The land surrounding it—all 800 acres of it and which had belonged to Billy's mother since her husband's passing in 2008—

was being sold to developers. For years Billy's parents had resisted selling the land to appease the county's desire to create a new suburb to Atlanta's evolving sprawl. The land was mostly forested hills and slopes, a favorite north Georgia destination for amateur hunters. Billy's sister's revelation that the land was to be sold required the approval and participation of both the estate and the foundation. Billy's success as a playwright coincided with his father's retirement and declining health and a rise in property taxes in the county. Billy had provided loans—and liens against the property—as means of assistance to his father—and his family—and now the estate and the foundation had the ability to prevent the sale of it.

A week later I was on a plane to Atlanta after consultations with lawyers and tax advisors, all of whom I felt certain would benefit more from this transaction than I or the estate or foundation would. Billy grew up in Galena, a small community in the piedmont area of north Georgia, in the foothills of the Appalachian Blue Ridge mountains. The house and land were a ninety-minute drive northeast of the airport. Once past the urban sprawl and the perimeter highways, squinting in the bright sunshine, the drive in the rental car was slow and hypnotic, nothing but highway lanes, hills and exits, and heat shimmers rising up from the concrete. As a born and bred New Englander it is always shocking to me how humid the South is and a mystery to me how anything of other than misery can benefit in this climate. Yet I'm always amazed that some of the most sophisticated people in my life have come from such hard Southern rural environments. Billy had an astonishing breadth of trivia of many subjects, from chemistry to archeology to pop culture. I've often wondered if this was because it had nothing to do with geographical roots, but of how information arrived to us in those days, news of the rest of the world was housed in books and encyclopedias, discovered at libraries, though magazine subscriptions, or broadcast into fuzzy black-and-white TV screens. I've often wondered how Billy would have reacted to the random and senseless information arriving rapidly through the technology of today, from the banal Facebook posts and Twitter feeds to selfies taken with smartphones.

Though Billy died in our apartment in New York City, he was buried in his family's plot in north Georgia. It was something he fiercely wanted and something I objected to silently, never believing that I would allow it to happen. "We might be able to tattoo our skin," Billy said, "but we don't lose our blood."

I hadn't been to Billy's grave in more than a decade, though the highway exit and the state road became familiar as soon as I reached them. The hardest thing of my life was to watch Billy go, and the next hardest was to let him rest in peace so far away from me, but I gave in to his request to be buried in his hometown, and it became another reason why I fought so hard to make the estate and the foundation into a living piece of memory.

I'd been aware of the drought that had begun in Georgia as far back as 2007, but by 2014 it was seldom on the news or discussed in information that I received, so I thought it had passed. As I drove closer to Galena, I was surprised to see the exposed, dry flat beds of the nearby lake and the red clay rims which the water level had covered and realized this area had never recovered—and was, in fact, still experiencing a record drought.

I found the cemetery and walked to Billy's grave on the slope of a hillside and left flowers. When I had allowed the burial to take place in the South, I made certain that the headstone would also carry the name Billy had chosen to write under. And there both names were recorded. William R. Graham and William B. Goodman. I'm not one of those visitors to cemeteries who ask the dead for advice—What should I do about the land? How should I treat your family? Billy's own opinions could go either way within the space of a millisecond. At times he was stubborn and combative, and other times he was the most gracious man I ever knew.

When I returned to the car, I called Janet from my cellphone. She repeated the instructions to the house, which I already knew, and I told her I would meet her there shortly.

The house was not completely empty, but the walls were bare, and the old furniture, now antiques—the pie safe, the china hutch, the long, handmade dining table—were gone. I realized that I should have inquired about them as well as part of the valuation of the property, but it was mid-day and the heat inside the house was stifling; sweat was rivering down my arms and back, and I did not want to walk in and begin with an argument.

The boxes had been left in the room that had once been Billy's bedroom—I had seen it when the funeral services had been held. It was now stripped of its identity. Janet plugged in a fan and I lifted the boxes to a folding table that had been set up and thumbed through the contents. I felt certain that Janet and her brothers had already looked inside and had taken anything they thought might be of value. Billy had once told me that after he left home for college, his siblings had acted as if he had died, raiding his room of his possessions—a portable stereo and speakers, a wireless radio, and the clothes he had left behind in his closet. Even the typewriter he had been given as a birthday present had ended up in the hands of his younger brother.

Inside the boxes were Billy's childhood documents, a copy of his birth certificate, a few boyhood photos, envelopes containing his grade school report cards and the medals he had earned in track competitions, college pamphlets and his SAT scores. If they had been my own I would have junked them—I'd lost my own sentimentality after Billy's death. But since they were Billy's, I thought they at least deserved more attention than an empty hot room afforded. As I was looking through the last of four boxes, Janet arrived with a shoe box. "I've held onto this as long as I want," she said. "You could take this too."

I opened the lid and saw that it was a jewelry box, a small leather box that a boy might own. I lifted the lid and looked at the odd assortment of items it held. Cuff links, a lanyard, a pocket knife, several sets of keys, and a ring. "That's his high school ring," Janet said.

I carried the boxes out to the car, thinking that I would consolidate them later at the nearby motel room I had booked. As I was carrying the last box to the car, a truck arrived in the driveway. It was Janet's husband, Andy. We greeted each other with a handshake.

To fill the awkwardness of the moment and the reunion, I made a comment which would change the direction of my visit. "I had forgotten that you could see the lake from the house," I said to Andy. "It's really a sore sight. All that dry land."

"Every year or so they find another car down there," he said. "Makes everyone in the county stinking mad cause all the hoopla keeps making taxes go up."

It was a casual remark, not intending to be newsworthy, and I laughed at its delivery, then looked at my watch. I had an appointment to meet an attorney in a half-hour's time. I asked about the location of the closing of the sale of the property—at another attorney's office close to the house in two days' time.

"I'm glad we could get this settled so quickly," Janet said.

I nodded and opened the car door. The buyer had delivered funds to an escrow account in the name of the estate for the removal of the liens, the purpose behind my meeting with the local lawyer. Arguments, however, had ensued over whether Billy—as a deceased person—was entitled to a percentage of the sale of the property. We had reached a settlement prior to my trip that would benefit and fund an endowment to the foundation—hence my presence at the closing to provide signatures. Fortunately, a confidentiality clause now limits the amount of bitter and complicated details I may disclose.

After meeting and signing documents at the attorney's office, I asked for directions to the local library. At the front desk, I asked a librarian if there was a clipping file of cars that had been discovered in the lake the last few years because of the drought. She gave me a curious look, as if I were a felon revisiting the scene of the crime, but she didn't ask for credentials or more information about myself. "There's a file on the Miller-Jackson case, about the two girls who disappeared in 1971. They were found last year. But the paper's been good about archiving everything," she said. "Lot of stuff online now. You could use one of the terminals to do a search."

Of course, I thought. An internet search. Why had I never thought about that all these years?

It took two days of reading articles, but before I left Galena I discovered that a car had been discovered wheels up in 2013. A boater had spotted the wheels poking up out of the water where a ravine sloped down to the lake, near Pine Point, almost five miles west.

The car, without a license tag, was so badly rusted out that the best investigators could estimate was that it was a black 1968 Mercedes. It took crews two days to clear a passage to pull it out of the ravine and the mud. At a news conference, the county sheriff said the badly decomposed remains of an unidentified man had been discovered in the trunk of the car. Fingerprints could not be found on the car or lifted from the remains of the body. The license plate had not been recovered.

To the dismay of the town, the state medical examiner's office had called in archeologists from the University of Georgia and forensic scientists from Atlanta to help piece together a timeline and the identity of the victim. It was estimated that the car had been submerged for more than thirty years. The body was determined to be male, possibly Hispanic, between 20 and 50 years old, with a height of about five-feet six inches.

"It could be years before the skeletal remains are positively identified," authorities said. Local records and the National Missing and Unidentified Persons System, a bureau of the Justice Department's National Institute of Justice, had not provided a missing persons match.

The county sheriff called it "an unsolved mystery until we prove otherwise."

And the mystery, however, does not begin and end here. A few weeks after I returned to Manhattan, I sorted through the boxes and found a few items that I felt should be archived with Billy's papers at the library, the rest I would place in a storage locker the foundation maintained. I had stored the shoebox and the jewelry box it held inside on a shelf in my closet. The day before I was scheduled to have dinner with Jameson Currier, who I knew would be eager to know the contents of the boxes as well as those of the jewelry box, I retrieved the shoebox from my closet. As I was looking at the high school ring—there was an inset letter G under the stone—probably for Galena High—the number of loose keys and key rings caught my attention and I thought I would examine them. I looked at several. The keys were duplicates, probably house keys, one opened a small lock that had also been in the box. One key ring had an inscription, "To WRG, Love SRP," probably from a high school girlfriend.

At the bottom of the box was another key ring—a thin, black leather strap with four keys. As I looked at the keys for some sign of identification—I noticed that the leather strap was embossed. As I ran my fingers over the letters and lifted it toward my eyes, the word "M E R C E D E S" emerged.

Two keys appeared to be car keys. Ignition. Doors and trunk. Along with two other keys, possibly to building doors.

I don't offer this as a mystery solved because another one immediately came into my mind: Why hadn't Billy thrown the keys away? Why had he left them behind to be found?

ACKNOWLEDGMENTS

The documents contained herein are artistic reproductions of originals now in the possession of the publisher. The publisher will comply with any legal request to review the original documents.

JAMESON CURRIER

Jameson Currier is the author of seven novels: *Where the Rainbow Ends, The Wolf at the Door, The Third Buddha, What Comes Around, The Forever Marathon, A Gathering Storm,* and *Based on a True Story*; five collections of short fiction: *Dancing on the Moon; Desire, Lust, Passion, Sex; Still Dancing: New and Selected Stories; The Haunted Heart and Other Tales*; and *Why Didn't Someone Warn You About Prince Charming?*; and a memoir, *Until My Heart Stops*. His most recent books are his illustrated tales, *Paul's Cat, The Candlelight Ghost, The Devil's Cake,* and *The Man That Got Away*. His short fiction has appeared in many literary magazines and Web sites, including *Velvet Mafia* and *Christopher Street,* and the anthologies *Men on Men, Best American Gay Fiction, Best Gay Stories, Wilde Stories, Unspeakable Horror,* and *Making Literature Matter*. In 2005, his AIDS-themed short stories were translated into French and published as *Les Fantômes* and in 2021, his novel, *The Third Buddha,* about the aftermath of 9/11 in Manhattan and Afghanistan, was translated into French by Étienne Gomez and published as *Le Troisième Bouddha* by Perspective cavalière and was awarded the Prix du Roman Gay. His reviews, essays, interviews, and articles on AIDS and gay culture have been published in many national and local publications, including *The Washington Post, The Los Angeles Times, Lambda Book Report, The Washington Blade, Bay Area Reporter, The New York Blade, Out,* and *Body Positive*. He is also the author of the documentary *Living Proof: HIV and the Pursuit of Happiness*. In 2010 he founded Chelsea Station Editions, an independent press devoted to gay literature. The press also serves as the home for Mr. Currier's own writings which now span a career of more than five decades. Books published by the press have been honored by the Lambda Literary Foundation, the American Library Association GLBTRT Roundtable, the Saints and Sinners Literary Festival, the Gaylactic Spectrum Awards Foundation, the Publishing Triangle, and the Rainbow Book Awards. In 2011, Mr. Currier launched the literary magazine *Chelsea Station*, and in 2014 relaunched the magazine as an online literary site. A self-taught artist, illustrator, and graphic designer, Mr. Currier's design work is tagged as "Peachboy" and his original art is signed "Jimmy." In 2020, he established Chatham Junction Studio, which serves as the curator for his expanding body of original art. Mr. Currier has been a member of the Board of Directors of the Arch and Bruce Brown Foundation, a recipient of a fellowship from New York Foundation for the Arts, and a judge for many literary competitions. He currently divides his time between a studio apartment in New York City and a farmless farmhouse in the Hudson Valley.

www.ingramcontent.com/pod-product-compliance
Lightning Source LLC
Chambersburg PA
CBHW051716280626
47162CB00018BC/2951